betrayal

chasing yesterday

book one . . . **awakening**
book two . . . **betrayal**
book three . . . **truth**

chasing yesterday

book two
betrayal

robin wasserman

SCHOLASTIC INC.

New York Toronto London Auckland Sydney
Mexico City New Delhi Hong Kong Buenos Aires

ISBN-13: 978-0-439-93341-4
ISBN-10: 0-439-93341-2

Book design by Tim Hall

12 11 10 9 8 7 6 5 4 3   7 8 9 10 11 12/0

Printed in the U.S.A.
First printing, July 2007

For Gina, who started it all.
For Randi, who believed in me.
For Bethany, who kept me from falling.
For Craig, who took a chance.

Thank you.

hunted

This time, there would be no escape.

The girl was close. He knew it. Even without the GPS-synced tracking device, he would have known. He didn't need the insistent blinking light that locked down her coordinates, closer, closer, closer still. He could *feel* her presence. He didn't need the machines any more than he needed the men, his cowardly troops gripping their tranquilizer guns, their eyes betraying their fear.

She was, after all, just a girl. She had power, true. But he had more.

Dangerous as she was — and now, lost, scared, out of control, she was more dangerous than ever — he had no doubt that he could find her and capture her. This was more than pride; this was certainty. He knew the girl better than anyone, knew what she was capable of. Knew her weaknesses and how to

1

use them. She was, after all, his creation, the pinnacle of his achievement; and he was her master. Despite recent setbacks, that was still true. That would always be true.

Only a few days before, he'd almost gotten past her defenses, almost drawn her back into the fold. Before, he'd done it on his own, without the trackers, without the men, without the guns.

But before, there had been time.

And now time was running out.

There was no margin for error. They would trap her before she had a chance to flee. Before she had a chance to fight.

Yes, his time was running out.

But so was hers.

"We're in range, sir," the voice in his headset reported. It was competent and level, as emotionless as a robot. And just as obedient. "Target is less than five hundred yards away. Our men are in position."

The doctor smiled.

He was known by many names. But he liked it best when they called him "sir," a note of respect in their voice, and beneath it, a tremble of fear. Awake, the girl had called him "Dr. Styron," and in the end, she had defied him. But asleep, under his control, she had called him "sir." And she had always obeyed.

Almost always, he reminded himself.

And the smile disappeared.

"Waiting for your signal," said the voice in his headset. He stared out the bulletproof tinted window of the SUV.

They were under orders not to hurt the girl. The boy who was with her was unwanted debris. No one would notice if he disappeared. But the girl was to be brought back intact. She was worth nothing to him dead.

He was prepared, everything was in place — and he had already waited too long.

"Go."

The sky glowed gray with the first light of dawn. A train rumbled on the elevated tracks overhead, but the wide street slept quiet and empty as the men in black swarmed, tranquilizer guns at the ready. They rounded the corner and advanced into the alley, movements stealthy and silent, weapons drawn, approaching from all sides. The prey was surrounded.

But the alley was empty.

"They've got to be here," one of them whispered, gesturing to the blinking light on his tracking monitor. These were the coordinates. The targets should be in place, cowering against the dank brick wall.

Silence broke into chaos as the men tore through Dumpsters, overturned garbage cans, knocked down doors, spread, searched, first annoyed, then mystified.

Then desperate.

And finally, too late, they found their answer.

The tracker had been implanted in a small silver heart, threaded through a chain, fastened around the girl's neck. To all appearances, an innocent gift from a loving mother.

A loving mother last seen lying unconscious amid advancing flames.

An innocence betrayed.

A gift left abandoned in the street.

A large gray rat nibbled at the thin silver chain, then clamped its teeth down on the heart and dragged it into the darkness. On the trackers, the small blinking light drifted across the screen, following the rat as it scurried through the scattered garbage. It ran out of the alley and down a sewer grate.

The men gaped at one another. The good news: They wouldn't have to face the girl. The bad, terrifying news: They would have to face the doctor.

"Sir, we have . . . a problem," the one in charge reported into the headset.

"Have you secured the girl?"

He knew telling the truth meant punishment, but lying would be worse. Lying meant destruction.

"No."

Impossible, he thought.

Yet it had happened. She had escaped. She was out there somewhere, beyond his grasp. She was running; she was winning.

This is all Dr. Mersenne's fault, he told himself. She had failed him again. He had wanted to bring the girl in immediately after the explosion, the moment they had located her, lost and confused in a local hospital. That was almost two weeks ago now, and he still had no idea what had gone wrong. The field test had proceeded perfectly — until the very end. And when the chaos cleared, the girl had lost her memory — and he had lost his control. At least, the girl *claimed* to have no memory of the past. He had no reason to trust that — and plenty of reasons to get her back to the Institute before things got worse.

But Dr. Mersenne had counseled patience. Dr. Mersenne, the only one he had ever trusted, the only one who could be counted on to be even more ruthless than he, had shown mercy. Had become an optimist overnight. He'd wanted to cut their losses, terminate the subject and cobble together a replacement for the defective merchandise; Dr. Mersenne insisted on maintaining hope. She had concocted the plan, persuaded him that the situation could still be salvaged, that the girl hadn't been damaged beyond repair. She could be retrained, reprogrammed, reclaimed — all in time to fulfill her purpose.

The ruthless Dr. Mersenne had put on a happy face, adopted a sweet, maternal gaze, had hugged her "daughter," had made promises of love and protection. Had lied, and lied well. She had fooled the media vultures. More important, she had fooled the girl. And even when progress was slow, she had urged patience. She had insisted that the project could be saved. Right up to the end, she had truly believed that.

And what had she gotten for her faith?

Burned.

He had been angry when he learned of the fire, angrier still when the men found Dr. Mersenne in the flames. When the final report came in, concluding that the girl was alive — and on the run — his rage had bubbled to the surface. Now it threatened to boil over.

But he refused to reveal himself in front of his men. So he painted on a smile.

The door to the SUV opened, and his chief lieutenant climbed into the driver's side. He turned toward the backseat, his eyes aimed steadily over the doctor's left shoulder.

The doctor had noticed this: People preferred not to look him in the eye.

"What now, sir?" There was a nearly undetectable tightness in the man's tone. A slight hesitation. "Should we start preparing one of the others for —"

"No!" the doctor snapped. Dr. Mersenne had been right about one thing. They needed the girl. She had always been their biggest success. And if he could get her back, *when* he got her back, she would deliver. "Everything will proceed according to plan.

We can't afford to tip off the client about our . . . slight detour."

"All due respect, sir, this is more than a 'detour.' She could be anywhere. If we don't find her soon, or if she remembers what she is and where she came from —"

"She won't remember," the doctor said firmly, leaning his head back against the smooth leather seat. He shut his eyes and forced the anger back down, sealing it with a layer of icy determination. "She doesn't know anything that can hurt us — and she doesn't know how to protect herself against us. We'll find her. It's a dangerous world out there for an innocent young girl," the doctor said, tapping his fingers against the glass. "Especially a girl with her . . . *special* skills."

"You ask me, the world's a whole lot more dangerous with *her* on the loose," the underling complained. "Look at what she did to Dr. Mersenne."

"She can't hurt us," the doctor said quickly. He preferred not to think of Mersenne, and the fire, and how quickly everything had gone wrong. It raised too many disturbing questions. Had he underestimated the girl? Overestimated his control over her? Mersenne's maternal act had been honed to perfection, and the treatment sessions had proceeded perfectly. There had been no indication that everything was about to fall apart. On the contrary: Everything had been in place for her return to the Institute.

It was the boy, he thought, the rage rising once again. It all would have worked out were it not for the boy. They could have prevented it from the start, could have gotten rid of the boy, avoided the trouble — if only they had known.

It was an oversight he would not make again.

"We'll get her back," he said, and there was no room for doubt in his voice. "She needs us just as much as we need her. It's only a matter of time before she figures that out."

She would reveal herself. Someone with her abilities couldn't stay invisible for long. She could run for now, but in the end she had nowhere to go. Eventually, she would get tired and sloppy. She would have to give up; she would have to give in.

And when she did, he would be waiting.

run

This has happened before, *J.D. thinks, and* she knows what will happen next, but she can't stop it, can't stop herself. Her mother lunges toward her, swinging the gun into position.

Not my mother, *J.D. thinks, and the words sound wrong, but she knows them to be true.*

A flame flickers atop her mother's torch; her face glows with reflected light.

The gun is pointing at Daniel.

J.D. reaches for her mother. The fear and rage bubble through her veins. A tingling heat prickles across her fore-arms and she spreads her fingers wide. A burning sensation shivers through them. There is a jolt, a surge of energy shooting through her body and out through her hands, and then her mother flies into the air and over the railing.

And J.D. is happy.

She knew exactly what she was doing and what would happen, and she is happy.

She wraps her hands around the railing and watches her mother tumble through the air. The scream ends only when the body thuds against the wooden floor. The hot boil of anger fades to a simmer, then stills, stretches out flat and calm, turns to ice. Her mother's body does not move.

J.D. knows it is a dream. But it is also a memory, and just as in life, the flaming torch lands next to her mother. The fire burns, and the flames spread, creeping closer and closer to the body.

The body of my mother, she thinks, though she knows the woman is not — was not — her mother.

She knows it is a dream, because in life, she shrieked and cried. In life, it was an accident. But now she is not confused, she is not horrified, she is not afraid. She is content, because the job is done. And it was no accident.

She knows it is a dream, because in life, the woman lay still as the flames danced closer. But now, her eyes pop open. J.D. wants to look away, needs to look away. But cannot.

Her mother's eyes are pale blue, iridescent. Just like the ones J.D. sees when she looks in the mirror. A trickle of blood runs down her mother's forehead. When she speaks, *her voice is no louder than a whisper, each word gasped out like a last breath. But J.D. can hear everything.*

"You were never my daughter," the woman rasps, and their eyes are still locked together. "You were no one."

A hand slapped down on her mouth before she could scream. Still caught up in the dream, J.D. lashed out. Her arm thudded against Daniel's chest. He held tight and, after a moment, she remembered where they were, and what she'd done. She stopped struggling. But she still wanted to scream.

The last ten days had been one long, uninterrupted nightmare. And as for her life before that . . . it was still a total blank. Ten days ago, J.D. had opened her eyes to find herself lying in the rubble of a mysterious explosion, with no idea how she'd gotten there or who she was.

All she'd wanted were answers — and all she'd gotten were lies. A name that didn't belong to her. A psychiatrist who had pumped her head full of fake memories. A mother who had tucked her in, hugged her tight . . . and then tried to kill her.

But I killed her first, J.D. reminded herself, staring down at her hands in disbelief. She remembered facing the woman in the abandoned farmhouse, just like in the dream. She remembered the struggle, and the gun, and the hot mixture of anger and fear and betrayal. She remembered the gun flying out of the woman's hand — and then the woman herself, thrown off her feet, pushed over the edge. Though the details were hazy, J.D. knew she hadn't touched the woman. And yet, somehow, she knew she was responsible for her fall.

For her death, J.D. thought, finally accepting that this was no nightmare, that the horrors of the night before were all true. Her mother was not her mother. J.D. had no mother. No home, no identity, no past. She was once again a Jane Doe — and now she was also a killer.

There hadn't been time last night to ask questions — they had been too busy running. They didn't know who was chasing them; they only knew that they had to get away.

They: J.D. and Daniel.

Daniel was the one person she could trust. The one thing that made sense in all of this. Her one friend, who stood by her, despite everything that had happened to them. Despite everything she'd done.

After they left the woman behind in the fire, they had hopped a train into the city, desperate to get away. The woman was dead, but the psychiatrist, Dr. Styron, was still out there. And once he found out what had happened, J.D. knew there would be no stopping him. Wherever she went, he would follow.

But not that night. That night, they escaped.

It was dark when they finally arrived in the city, and they sought refuge in the cavernous train station with its hidden alcoves and dark corners. Daniel had fallen asleep immediately, his knees curled up tight against his chest, his arms shielding his face. But J.D. had stayed awake for hours, staring at her hands.

She wasn't my mother, J.D. told herself now, over and over again. She pressed her hand against her bare neck, where the heart necklace had hung. "A reminder of how much I love you," the woman had said with her lying smile. And J.D. had been stupid enough to believe her.

The night before, she had ripped it off her neck and tossed it off the speeding train. But it felt like it was still there, the metal chain cold against her skin, strangling her.

"It's starting to fill up," Daniel said, nodding toward the people wandering across the station's main concourse. "We should get out of here, but first —" He jumped to his feet and winked at her. She smiled weakly, wondering how, after all this, he could still pretend everything was okay. "I'll be right back."

She pressed herself back into the corner, half hidden from sight by a marble pillar that had probably been white a long, long time ago.

Daniel is coming back, she told herself. *You're not alone.*

He hadn't gone far, just across the concourse, where he seemed to be arguing with the owner of a small bakery stand. But it was far enough. If anything happened — if Dr. Styron was following them . . .

She wondered how fast she could run, if she needed to. She wondered how loud she could scream.

And then Daniel was back, a small paper bag in hand. He pulled out a bagel, broke it in two, and handed her the larger half. "It's rock hard," he warned, "or they wouldn't have given it away, but —"

"It's food," J.D. said, around a mouthful of stale but delicious bread. She hadn't realized how hungry she was. Or how grateful she was to have Daniel by her side.

"Also, I grabbed this out of the recycling bin,"

Daniel said. "I don't know if you want to see it, but . . ." He handed her a soggy, wrinkled newspaper, folded over to an inside page. The headline read:

Tragic Fire Claims Girl Without a Past

"The Girl Without a Past," that's what the reporters had called her, after the explosion.

The doctors had called her Jane Doe.

She had named herself J.D., and that was the name that stuck. She was J.D., despite her "mother's" lies, despite Dr. Styron insisting that she call herself Alexa, her "real" name. Now she wondered about Dr. Styron's real name, and his real agenda. The whole time she'd been trusting him, believing he could help her remember the past, he had been tampering with her mind, implanting false memories, training her to love and trust the woman who was not her mother. Dr. Styron was the answer. But she still didn't know why.

According to the article, only one body was recovered from the burned-out shell of the abandoned building. Laura Collins, successful computer programmer, widow, single mother of one.

The body of her daughter, thirteen-year-old Alexa Collins, was not reclaimed. She, too, is presumed dead.

Alexa is *dead*, J.D. thought.

For too long, she had struggled to reclaim her old life, to force herself to be someone else. But there had never been an Alexa Collins. The name was as fake as the memories, as fake as her mother. And now J.D. didn't have to try anymore. She didn't have to pretend to be someone she wasn't.

She could just be J.D. The girl without a past.

Longtime family friend Dr. Warren Styron calls the fire a terrible tragedy. "We were all so thankful to get Alexa back safe and sound, and now for something like this to happen . . ." The psychiatrist choked up and had to take a break before continuing the interview.

Investigators have yet to uncover an explanation for the explosion that took down three city blocks almost two weeks ago. Alexa Collins, the only witness, suffered only minor injuries, but doctors say she exhibited a severe case of

retrograde amnesia, remembering nothing before her rescue from the explosion site. For
several days, her identity remained unknown.

After a brief hospital stay, Collins spent two
days at the Chester Center for Juvenile Services
before her mother, Laura Collins, arrived to
claim her.

"Laura was overjoyed," Dr. Styron said. "And
although Alexa had no memory of her mother,
the two of them obviously still shared a bond.
There was love there, anyone could see it." Dr.
Styron cited the harrowing days after Alexa went
missing. "Laura couldn't help fearing the worst,
but I told her that Alexa was strong, and she'd
come back to us — and I still believe that. There's
a chance she's still out there. And if she is, I'll
find her."

"Hey, it's going to be okay," Daniel said softly,
putting a hand on her shoulder.

He thought she was crying, J.D. realized. He
thought she was shaking with fear. But it wasn't
fear — it was anger.

"There's a chance she's still out there," Dr. Styron,
or whoever he was, had said. It was a message, a

message to J.D. He knew she wasn't dead — and he wasn't ready to let her go.

"It doesn't matter," she said, brushing Daniel away. "We've just got to get out of here."

"And go where? We can't just show up at the Center, even if we wanted to. They think you're Alexa. And we can't go to the cops." He tapped his finger against the article, resting it beneath three ugly words.

Police suspect arson.

The article didn't contain the word "murder." That one was only in J.D.'s head.

"I don't care where we go," J.D. said, inching farther back into their dark corner. The train station was swarming with commuters, strange faces that stared blankly ahead, but any one of them might have been searching for her. And J.D. wouldn't allow herself to be found. They had to run. "If we stay here, they'll find us, I know it."

"Who's going to find us?" Daniel asked. He tapped the paper again. "It says it right here, everyone thinks you're dead. That Styron guy probably gave up and crawled back to his evil lair. He and the rest of the supervillains are probably sitting around

19

watching TV and planning their next world take-over." He grinned, but she couldn't bring herself to smile back. He didn't understand. Even though he'd been with her, by her side through everything, he still didn't get it.

Maybe because he hadn't seen the video, the one that showed her lying hypnotized and helpless while Dr. Styron reshaped her mind. Daniel wasn't the one whose nightmares came to life during the day in vivid hallucinations of smoke, fire, and death. He wasn't the one who had no memory of the past; he hadn't spent the past week wondering whether or not he was crazy.

"*He's* still out there looking for me," she said. "Dr. Styron. I just — somehow, I just know it."

Daniel grimaced. "Like you just 'know' you some-how pushed your — the woman over the railing, even though you never touched her?"

"I *do* know."

And you know it, too, she thought. She had seen the look in his eyes, after it had happened. "What did you do?" he had asked, and she'd heard the fear in his voice.

Even if he didn't want to believe it now, he *knew*.

"J.D., you're not making any sense. There's no

20

way it was your fault. You were all woozy, whatever they drugged you with was wearing off, and I know what you think happened, but —"

"But I just imagined it?" she asked sourly.

"Don't you think that's more possible than —" Daniel glanced down at her hands, and she tucked them farther into her lap, like she was trying to hide a weapon — "than you having some kind of weird superpower?"

She didn't say anything.

"Okay, fine." He pursed his lips. "Let's say you do have some kind of, uh, power. Show me."

"What?"

"Show me," he said again. "Do something." He held up the paper bag. "Rip this in half or something. With your *miiiiiiiind*."

"That's not how it works," she snapped, staring at her hands, wondering if maybe that *was* how it worked. But she was too embarrassed to try.

"How do you know?"

"Because it's *my* —" She stopped. *It's my power,* she had been about to say. But even she knew that would have sounded ridiculous. The whole thing was impossible to believe. She wouldn't believe it, either, if she hadn't felt it. "Whatever. Never mind."

He leaned his head close to hers. "I know you feel guilty," he said, his tone softer. "But it wasn't your fault. She was chasing us, she was going to hurt you, she was going to hurt us both, and . . . it was just an accident."

"We could have gone back for her," she said quietly. "We could have pulled her out of the fire."

"There wasn't any time. There *wasn't*. And besides . . ."

"What?"

He looked like he didn't want to say it, but then he did. "Do you really think she would have gone back for *you*?"

J.D. didn't respond. She was staring at the man, the one on the other side of the atrium dipping a wedge of his doughnut into a cup of coffee. He wore a light brown jacket and had a folded-up newspaper tucked under his elbow. He couldn't have looked more normal. Except that he was watching her.

She knew she was being paranoid. But she had learned to trust her instincts.

J.D. caught the man's eye, expecting him to turn away. But instead, he smiled, lifted a cell phone to his ear, and began striding across the concourse. His steps were slow at first, almost casual, until J.D. stood up, tugging Daniel to his feet. Then the man began to walk faster, pushing through the crowd of commuters, heading straight for J.D.

"We have to get out of here," she hissed, pulling Daniel down the corridor, ducking into a stairwell.

"What? What are you doing?"

J.D. risked a glance over her shoulder, and for a moment thought they were safe. Then the man's face appeared through the crowd, and he was closer than before.

J.D. ran.

search

"Watch out!" a woman shouted as J.D. hurtled past. An armful of packages flew into the air, but J.D. kept running, pushing through a crowd of shoulders and elbows, her heart pounding as she raced down the hall, searching for an exit. The train station was massive, towering pillars stretching up to a vaulted roof, its tiles painted with crumbling images of the past. J.D. ran by gate after gate, skidded around a coffee vendor, then ducked behind a magazine stand as a security guard bustled toward her. Daniel crouched by her side.

"What are we doing?" he hissed. J.D. pressed her finger to her lips.

The guard spotted them. "You kids get back here!"

"We're running," J.D. gasped and took off again, pulling Daniel along after her. She didn't know if the man was still following them, but she couldn't risk waiting to find out.

Finally, she caught sight of a red EXIT sign. She pushed open the door before she could read the fine print: EMERGENCY EXIT: WARNING, ALARM WILL SOUND.

A siren blared, and a red light over the door began to flash. J.D. froze, the light splashing across her face. There was something about the way it flickered, something strange. Something familiar.

She stopped running. Stopped moving. Stared at the light.

The world around her seemed to fade. Nothing was important; nothing mattered. She could relax. She could float away from her body, give up control.

Soon the order would come, tell her what to do next, and she would obey.

She waited.

"J.D.!" Daniel grabbed her roughly and pulled her through the door. "If we're running, let's *run*!"

For a moment, J.D. was lost. The world had sped up again, burst into noise and light and color, and the panic surged through her body. But her mind was still a step behind, trapped in the weird state of calm. She was frozen.

Then it was over, and she was jolted out of it, back to the world — back to herself.

What was *that?* she thought, shuddering. But there was no time to figure it out, no time to think at all.

Daniel took off to the right, racing to the corner and then making a sharp turn down a broad avenue filled with cars and people and noise. J.D. followed, quickly losing any sense of direction as he wound them around corner after corner, darting across streets and zigzagging around clumps of people clogging the sidewalks.

J.D. ran with her head down, trusting Daniel to lead their way, so she didn't look up as they raced across the street against the light. She didn't see the taxi barreling toward her. Someone shouted, and the brakes screamed and squealed, and only then, finally, she did look up.

The blur of yellow filled her field of vision, grinding toward her, brakes screeching, but it was still coming at her, too big and too fast — and then Daniel dragged her out of the way. The bumper grazed her shirt as the car tore through the intersection. For a moment, J.D. didn't understand why she wasn't lying on the ground, broken and bleeding. Daniel was still holding on to her, his grip so tight it hurt.

She touched her hand to her left side, where the car had brushed against her. If Daniel had been a second slower, if the car had swerved in the other direction . . .

"You okay?" he asked, his face pale.

Don't think about it, she told herself. *Just don't think about what could have happened. Not now.* So she nodded. Daniel looked like he didn't believe her.

J.D. turned away, scouring the faces clustering around them. The man who'd been chasing them was gone. "I think we're safe," she whispered, but there were too many people staring at them, and they were starting to ask questions. How long would it be before someone called the cops about the poor little girl who almost got hit by a car? Or before someone recognized her from the papers?

And even if they could get away, if they kept running, how long could it last? It was only a matter of time before someone caught them and dragged them back to Dr. Styron. Then what?

"We should split up," she said suddenly.

"What?" Daniel took her arm and guided her to a nearby bench. They sat down on the edge of a small plaza dotted with dogs and strollers and couples strolling arm in arm, enjoying the sun. J.D. pressed her hands against her face, partly to hide herself away and partly because she didn't want to see. All those people with their normal lives, nothing to worry about but where to go for lunch . . . she felt a sudden rush of anger. She hated them, hated their boring problems and their careless happiness.

And all she wanted was to be one of them.

For the first time, she let herself mourn Alexa Collins, the girl she might have been. The happy girl smiling back at her from all the doctored photos, her arms around her friends, her face tilted back in laughter. J.D. had escaped the fire, but Alexa had burned there, right alongside her mother. Alexa Collins was dead, and so was any hope for a normal past or a normal life. J.D. was trapped in her nightmare now — but Daniel, at least, could wake up.

"You should go back to the Center," she told him, staring down at her hands. "It won't be so bad. You'll be fifteen soon, and maybe you can get into that work-release program and go live somewhere else, be on your own, and it'd be okay. . . ."

"I'm not leaving you," he said indignantly. "I told you I'd stick with you, whatever happened, and I *will*. We're in this together now."

"We're *not*," she said, turning toward him. His

cheeks were red, and the wind was blowing his brown hair straight up into billowing spikes. "Whatever Styron wants, he's after me, not you. This is too dangerous."

"Too dangerous for me, but not too dangerous for you?" he asked. "I know you're not suggesting you're tougher than me." Giving her a cocky grin, he raised his fists. "You want to settle this right now?"

"Stop messing around!" She smacked his arm in frustration. "Daniel, this isn't your fight." Across the plaza, a little kid bundled up in a thick winter coat climbed over the concrete ledge and into the dry fountain. "And if anything happens to you . . . Please. Just go back, go somewhere safe. Let me deal with this."

The little boy's mother shouted something incoherent, then scooped him up, dragging him out of the fountain, back to the safety of the playground. The children were shrieking as they clambered over the playground equipment; from where J.D. was sitting, the piercing screeches seemed violent.

Daniel's crooked smile faded away, and the dimple above his cheek disappeared. "Go back where?" he asked softly. "To the Center? Let them kick me around some more, tell me what to do? Or maybe

I'll get *really* lucky and get shipped off to another foster family, some new bunch of —" He cut himself off and shook his head. "I don't have anything," he said, his grip tightening on the edge of the bench until his knuckles turned white. "Don't you get that? I don't have anything to go back to. I don't have anything . . . except *this*. For the first time ever, I'm doing something that matters, and I've got someone who actually needs me around —"

"I don't need you," she protested.

"Yeah, you do." The corners of his lips twitched, like the smile was just beneath the surface, struggling to break through. "Even if you don't want to admit it. So I'm not ditching you, get it? Say whatever you want, but I'm staying."

"Things are going to get bad," she warned him. There was a sense of doom weighing her down, like it was only a matter of time before —

But that was the problem. Before what? She didn't know, couldn't remember. But it felt like somewhere, in the back of her mind, behind a thick wall of fog, lay the answer. Some part of her knew why she was being chased, knew what they wanted from her, and knew exactly what would happen if she got caught.

And that part was terrified.

"Things are already bad," Daniel pointed out.

"Worse," she said. "It's going to get worse."

Daniel grinned. "It always does." He stood up, grabbed her hands, and pulled her off the bench. "Come on."

"Come where?"

"To get some answers," he said. "Then let's see how they like it when *we* chase *them*."

Their hunt began in the basement of the nearest public library, where a few ancient computers were available for public use. J.D. sat perched on the edge of her chair, her finger hovering over the mouse, her muscles clenching as she clicked through to each Google entry for *Dr. Warren Styron*. Daniel hovered behind her, holding his breath with each link, as they waited for the page to open. The connection was painfully slow, but J.D. forced herself to sit still, forced herself to wait, forced herself to hope.

Until finally, after they'd clicked through more than fifty useless results, J.D. was forced to admit that Styron was a dead end.

There was a Warren Styron who practiced orthopedic surgery in Los Angeles.

A Warren Styron who had died in 1948 from injuries suffered in a tractor collision.

Warren Styron, MD, whose revolutionary cure for male pattern baldness could be yours for only $49.99 plus shipping and handling.

Warren Styron, SWM, whose hobbies included tennis and gourmet cooking, seeking SWF for "long moonlit walks and cuddling by the fire."

But none of the Warren Styrons was a psychiatrist specializing in hypnotherapy; none of them lived on the right coast or had the right photo. None was *her* Dr. Styron.

"This isn't going anywhere," Daniel finally whispered, rubbing his eyes. Most of the bulbs in the basement had burned out, and the old screens were dim and dusty enough that both of them had to squint. "Maybe we should try pulling up articles about the explosion. Or photos. We still don't know what you were doing there in the first place, right? There's got to be some kind of clue, evidence, something."

"Good idea," J.D. said. But she had her own idea, and she didn't want Daniel to know what she was thinking. Not yet. "This is stupid, using just one computer." She nodded toward one of the other computers. "Divide and conquer?"

Once Daniel was gone, J.D. turned back to the keyboard and, feeling a little silly, entered in a new set of search terms.

mind control
brainwashing
moving things with your mind
powers
memory loss

There were plenty of results. Thousands of them. Wackjob conspiracy theorists posting about massive government mind control schemes. New Age healers preaching about unlocking the hidden powers of the mind. The sites were weird, unsettling, laughable, and almost entirely useless.

Almost, but not quite.

She clicked open an article titled "Research Suggests Genetic Predisposition for Telekinesis" and sucked in a breath as she read about the work of a geneticist named Ansel Sykes. He claimed that certain genetic sequences could produce unusual "parapsychological" abilities — specifically, telekinesis, the power to move things with the mind. Some years earlier, Sykes had presented his work at a national genetics conference. He admitted that his subjects showed extremely limited telekinetic abilities, so limited as to appear nonexistent to other researchers. But he claimed that a combination of practice and medication could, hypothetically, enhance these natural abilities. Sykes speculated that, given a rigorous screening process, intensive training, and the right drug protocol, he would be able to "unlock the hidden potential of the human brain and create a new human form, one with limitless possibilities." He had been laughed off the stage.

The article was more than two decades old. J.D. searched for something more recent, but the conference had apparently been Ansel Sykes's last public appearance. After his humiliating lecture, Dr. Sykes had disappeared.

And then she found it, a small blurb in the city paper from almost fifteen years ago, noting that a local geneticist had been awarded a grant from a company named LysenCorp. The grant was for more than a million dollars, the research was "confidential," and no one seemed to know what the company did, other than lavish money on eccentric researchers who quickly disappeared from public view.

J.D. scrolled down, hungry for more — and gasped. There was a picture accompanying the article, a head shot of the young geneticist. The caption read, "Ansel Sykes, the latest scientist to land a wind-fall from the mysterious LysenCorp, is regarded by many in his field as a purveyor of flimsy pseudo-science."

J.D. stared at the photo. It was him. Even with the grainy black-and-white photo, even with the face that was fifteen years younger than the one she knew, she was sure. It was him. Dr. Styron.

Ansel Sykes, she thought, turning the name over in her mind.

She knew the name of her enemy.

Twenty years ago, he had talked of screening the population, finding those rare individuals whose genes gave them special abilities. He had talked of seeking the key to the brain's hidden powers.

What if he had found it?

What if he had found *her*?

"Daniel," she called out in a strangled voice, for-getting to whisper. "I think I found something."

"What?"

But by the time Daniel came over, J.D. had clicked open another site. The LysenCorp home page offered no information about what the company did or where it was located. There were no links to personnel pages or a corporate directory. There was only a bland paragraph about "maximizing earning potential and seeking future growth" centered beneath the corporate logo. But it was enough.

J.D. couldn't speak. She couldn't breathe. She leaned toward the screen, pressing her fingers against the black icon.

Daniel gasped.

"Unbelievable." His hand grazed the back of her neck, pausing at the spot where her shoulder blades met. J.D. knew what he was staring at. The tiny black tattoo, the one she had no memory of getting, the strange symbol that she couldn't get out of her mind:

She had been marked with the LysenCorp logo.

No, that wasn't the right word for it, she thought, pressing her hand against the tattoo. It felt cold beneath her fingertips.

She had been *branded*.

underground

"What are you kids doing here?" an angry voice boomed from the doorway. "Shouldn't you be in school?"

J.D. turned slowly. A woman in her fifties stood in the doorway, her brown hair falling limply across her shoulders and her lips pursed. The reindeer leaping across her thick green sweater looked like it was about to eat her face.

"We're here for a school project, ma'am," Daniel said quickly, reaching across J.D. to shut down her browser. "We have special permission."

The librarian nodded. Her eyes narrowed. "I've seen you before," she said, staring at J.D. "I know you."

J.D. shook her head, wishing her hair was long enough to hide behind.

"We're done with our research," Daniel said,

standing up. J.D. jumped up beside him. "So we should probably just . . ."

They inched toward the doorway.

The woman blocked their path. "It's *you*."

"We have to go," Daniel said urgently, and though he appeared to be speaking to the librarian, J.D. knew better. She nodded, and tried to squeeze past the woman, whose bulk filled up the doorway. A clammy hand locked down on her arm.

"You're the girl from the papers," the librarian said excitedly. "The one who's supposed to be dead." J.D. tried to rip her arm away, but the woman held tight.

"Let go!" She suddenly realized that Daniel was gone. He'd left her behind, left her on her own. "I don't know who you think I am, but I'm not her, I'm no one. I just have to get out of here."

"Oh, no." The woman laughed mirthlessly. "You're coming with me."

Anger bubbled up inside of J.D., and she felt it, that familiar warm heat flooding through her body, the rush of power and the temptation to seize control.

The librarian's grip tightened on her arm as she dragged J.D. up the stairs and across the front hall, toward the security desk. J.D. flexed her fingers, preparing for . . . something.

Her mother flies through the air, tumbling head over heels over head, until the thud.

The body lies bloody and still.

J.D. took a deep breath and forced the rage back down, deep inside her, until the tingling faded away and the heat receded. She couldn't hurt anyone like that, not again. No matter what it cost her.

The librarian pushed her up against the security desk, where a bored-looking guard was reading a comic book. "You're never going to believe who I —"

The fire alarm cut the woman off in midsentence. Her grip on J.D.'s arm loosened, just for a moment, but it was enough. J.D. slipped out of her grasp and raced for the front exit. She pushed through the heavy brass door and raced down the stairs, toward the end of the block, around a corner — and then stopped, taking a deep breath. The air was bitter cold and tasted like smog, but she didn't care. She was free, she was safe, and she hadn't hurt anyone.

This time, at least.

"That's two you owe me," Daniel said, popping

up behind her. "If I rescue you one more time, do I win some kind of prize?"

Of course he hadn't left her behind. He would never do that to her. He'd promised.

"*You* pulled the alarm?"

Daniel nodded. "Always wanted to try that. Just needed a good excuse."

J.D. rubbed the back of her neck, running her fingers across her tattoo, wishing she'd had a chance to learn about LysenCorp and Ansel Sykes. Now that the librarian knew she was alive, it was only a matter of time before word spread. The police would be looking for her, and they wouldn't be the only ones. She was going to have to be a lot more careful. She was going to have to be invisible.

"Now would be when you thank me," Daniel prompted her.

"Uh, thanks," J.D. murmured, wondering: If Dr. Styron — Ansel Sykes — had been training her to use the strange powers in her mind, what was she supposed to be using them *for*?

"Your overwhelming gratitude means so much," Daniel teased, clapping a hand over his heart.

She remembered her mother — *not my mother,*

she reminded herself angrily — warning her that she was dangerous. Out of control. That everyone would be safer with her out of the way.

In the library, the rage had clouded her mind, and it had been so tempting to let herself lose control and unleash whatever power she had inside of her.

And then there was the dream she'd been having ever since the explosion — or was it a hallucination? A memory? A vision, vivid and too real, of standing in an empty field, raising her hands to the sky as the helicopter hovered overhead. She remembered the propeller snapping, the crash, the fire. She remembered choking on the smoke. She remembered Dr. Ansel Sykes by her side, congratulating her on a job well done.

She *was* dangerous. And for the first time, it occurred to her that maybe Sykes wasn't the bad guy. Maybe her "mother" hadn't been, either. Maybe they were just trying to keep people safe — safe from J.D.

Maybe she was the real enemy.

And maybe she should have let them stop her.

"That's crazy!" Daniel exclaimed.

J.D. bristled. It was a word she didn't like very

much. Not after being tranquilized and strapped into a straitjacket. Not after spending so many sleepless nights wondering if she was losing her mind. And Daniel knew it.

"I don't mean *you're* crazy," he said quickly. "I just mean you can't be right about all this. Not possible."

They were sitting in a movie theater lobby, according to Daniel one of the best places to escape the cold without spending any money. A few feet away, a huge poster promised "An adventure you'll never forget!" The woman on the poster was dangling from a bridge, one hand clutching a metal railing, the other flailing wildly. She was smiling.

She could afford to smile. It was a movie, which meant her fingers wouldn't slip. She wouldn't fall to her death. She wouldn't break her neck when she slammed into the water or sink beneath the surface after hours of treading water, her muscles exhausted, her hope gone, her body ready to give in. It was a movie, which meant she'd get her happy ending.

"First of all, you're not dangerous," Daniel said. J.D. had just finished telling him her theory. "And whoever's following us, they're *not* the good guys.

We are. Obviously. Second of all, you can't move things with your mind. No one can."

"What about the fight with Mel?" J.D. asked, reminding him of the girl at the Center who'd attacked J.D. and ended up crashing into the pavement, breaking her collarbone. J.D. hadn't touched her. She was sure of it.

"What *about* Mel?" Daniel countered. "You were upset, your adrenaline was flowing, and we all know you're tougher than you look."

Tougher, maybe. But tough enough to take on a kid who was almost a foot taller than her? A girl who carried a knife and knew how to use it?

"And my mother?" J.D. pressed.

Daniel sighed. "I was there, and I promise you, that *wasn't your fault*. I know you feel guilty about it, but you've really got to let it go."

"It's not just guilt," she said. She needed him to understand. Through it all, Daniel had stood by her, believing her when no one else did. He was the only person who hadn't betrayed her trust, and she needed him with her on this. "I know it sounds insane, but I can feel it inside of me, and it fits with all the visions or nightmares or whatever those were. There's something . . . not normal. And why else would Dr. Sykes be after me? What else could make me so valuable to him?"

Daniel jerked his head toward the nearby concession stand, where a giant neon sign taunted them with candy bars and popcorn. "Okay, Wonder Woman, if you've got these special powers, how about using them to get us something to eat?"

"I told you before, it doesn't work that way," J.D. said, blushing. She knew how ridiculous she sounded — and it would be easier to believe Daniel, to accept that there had to be a rational, normal explanation for everything. But she knew better.

"Then I vote we save the argument for later and move on to something more important," Daniel suggested.

"Like what?"

He nodded toward her stomach, which rumbled right on cue. "Dinner."

"Excuse me, miss, but there's a girl in the bathroom who seems really sick," J.D. told the girl behind the concession stand. She tried to look sweet, young, and clueless, just as Daniel had advised. The older girl, still examining her zits in the reflection of the soda machine, just looked bored. "She's throwing up all over and she's, like, really pale and weak. Can you come help her?"

The girl rolled her eyes and sighed loudly. "Like I'm a doctor or something," she muttered, but she came out from behind the concession stand and followed J.D. to the bathroom. "I'm *not* cleaning up some kid's puke," she said, holding her breath as the door swung open.

The bathroom was empty. "Oh, I don't know where she went." J.D. tried to sound shocked and apologetic. She opened her eyes wide, scratched the side of her head. "Maybe she got better? Sorry to bother you."

"Whatever." The older girl rolled her eyes and, instead of leaving the bathroom, went over to the mirror and began reapplying her lip gloss. J.D. just stood in the doorway and watched. *Maybe she has a date tonight,* she thought. *Or maybe she has a crush on one of the ushers. Maybe she just likes to look good.* From where she was standing, J.D. could see her own reflection in the mirror, next to the girl's. It was the opposite of good: filthy and bedraggled. She'd been wearing the same clothes for two days — if she were a comic strip character, there would have been squiggly stink lines blasting off of her. J.D. tried to picture herself primping in front of a mirror, smoothing down her glossy hair and smearing on some glittery eye shadow. She couldn't.

"What?" the girl snapped, without tearing her eyes from her reflection. "You got a problem?"

J.D. shook her head silently, then backed away. As planned, she left the theater and hurried up the block and around the corner. Daniel was supposed to be there waiting for her, but he wasn't. She waited, feeling a little queasy.

As the minutes passed and he still didn't appear, she forced herself not to worry. Tried not to imagine him getting caught behind the concession stand, his hands clenching fistfuls of candy. Tried not to picture the cops dragging him away and throwing him in jail, his life ruined, all because he'd stuck with J.D.

"Dinner is served, madame!" Daniel called out, tossing her a candy bar as he rounded the corner. She caught it on reflex, but for a moment she was too relieved to process anything but the fact that Daniel was safe. They'd gotten away with it.

Then she looked down at the chocolate in her hands, and the hunger knocked all other thoughts out of her head. She tore open the wrapper and crammed the candy bar into her mouth, moaning with pleasure as something finally filled up the emptiness inside. For several long minutes, they stuffed their faces in silence.

"Told you this would work," Daniel mumbled around a mouthful of Reese's Peanut Butter Cup. "And it went even better than I thought." He reached into his coat pocket and pulled out a fistful of something green, then opened his hand to reveal a small pile of bills.

J.D. felt like all the chocolate in her stomach was going to rush back up her throat. "Where did you get that?"

"Where do you think?"

J.D. grabbed the money out of his hands. "You said you were just going to take food," she said angrily. "Because we needed it. I don't steal."

"I said I was going to *steal* food because we needed it," Daniel said, his voice rising. "So yeah, *we* steal. And we need *this,* too."

"We can't just go around stealing from people, not even if we need it."

"You got a better idea?" Daniel asked. "Do you have some secret bank account I don't know about?

You have a job? Where were you planning to sleep tonight, and the next night? What are you planning to eat?"

"I — I don't know."

"That's right, you *don't* know," Daniel said, and he snatched the money back from her and stuffed it into his pocket. "You don't know how hard things can get —"

"Yeah, because my life has been *so* easy up till now," J.D. snapped.

"You don't know *what* your life has been," Daniel said, "because you can't remember. But I do. I know what it's like. And I know what we need to survive."

J.D. leaned against the storefront and tipped her head back. She closed her eyes. "So *that's* your plan?" she asked. "We just keep running, and keep stealing, telling ourselves we're only doing what we need to do? What happens next? We just do this forever, or . . . until we get caught?"

Daniel leaned next to her. "It won't be like this forever," he said, his voice softer. "We just need some time to figure things out. And we will figure them out. No one's going to catch us." He paused. "It's only a few dollars. Just enough for more food tomorrow. But if you want, we could go back to the movie theater and leave the money in the lobby. I don't know if it's safe to go back there now, they might be looking for us, but if it matters that much to you . . ."

She opened her eyes. Daniel was hunched over against the cold, his head tucked into his chest, his eyes fixed on the pavement. She hated feeling this way, totally clueless about how to survive and what to do next. She didn't like following along behind Daniel, letting him tell her what to do and how to do it. She was too strong for that; she was too proud.

But when it came to things like this, Daniel knew what he was talking about. And proud or not, the smart thing to do was to listen.

"Not yet," J.D. said. "We'll pay them back — we have to — but not until it's safe. Not until *you* think it's safe."

Daniel raised his eyebrows. "Since when am I in charge?"

"Since never," J.D. said, laughing. "It's not about being in charge, it's about you knowing stuff that I don't. And if you say we need to do something . . ."

She didn't want to be here, shivering in the cold, making these decisions. She wanted to be somewhere warm and safe, somewhere normal. But it wasn't about what she wanted anymore. It was about staying hidden, and staying alive. "I trust you," she told him, and then she stopped talking, even though that was only half of what she wanted to say. She shoved her hands in her pockets.

I trust you. She wanted to tell Daniel, *Right now I trust you more than I trust myself.*

sanctuary

The wooden boards shuttering the windows rattled in the wind. J.D. tucked her arms inside her shirt and pressed them to her skin for warmth. Her jacket was balled up beneath her head, a lumpy pillow against the cold and dirty tile floor. Daniel had offered her his coat to use as a blanket, but she'd refused. And in the dim moonlight, she could see him shivering.

Something scrabbled in the darkness. J.D. imagined she could see tiny eyes gleaming from the shadows. *Rats,* she thought. Of course there would be rats.

A soft, insistent scratching.

Something skittered across the floor.

Or maybe cockroaches. That was even worse than rats. At least rats had fur and tails, like cats or puppies. Not nearly as cute, maybe, and with sharper teeth, teeth that would sink into your skin, chomp out tiny bites of flesh. She shivered. But still, cockroaches were worse. They weren't animals, they were monsters. That hard black shell, those long antennae, the spindly body . . . she tried not to picture skittering hordes of them, inky splotches crawling out of the walls, marching across the floor, seeking the warmth of human flesh. J.D. curled up into a tight ball, trying not to imagine tiny legs creeping across her in the night. Something feathered against her ankle, and she kicked out her leg, but there was nothing there. Just her imagination.

The room smelled like garbage, the stench heavy and almost sweet. When they'd first pushed their way inside — the door was hanging half off the hinges — J.D. had almost choked. The bile had risen in her throat, spilling a sour taste onto her tongue. But they'd been searching for an hour, and the abandoned apartment was the best spot they'd found. After a few minutes, they'd almost gotten used to the smell. She could forget about it for long stretches of time, and then it would return without warning, a wave of nausea sweeping over her and ebbing away again.

"Cold?" Daniel asked, his voice floating through the dark.

"Not really," J.D. lied. He'd been so proud of himself for leading them to this neighborhood with its empty streets and burned-out buildings, so proud of discovering the empty apartment, a place to pause, to hide, to sleep. She didn't want him to hear the disgust in her voice or know how much she hated the way her skin felt caked with layers of grime, her hair greasy and tangled into knots. This was hard. Harder than she'd expected. "Hey, can I . . . can I ask you something?"

"No."

"Oh." J.D. didn't know what to say. "Uh, sorry, I —"

"Kidding." She could hear the smile in his voice. "What is it?"

She had wanted to ask him all day, but now, in the dark, it seemed easier. "How do you know all this stuff?" she asked. "Where to find a place to sleep, and good places to get food, and . . . you know."

Daniel didn't say anything.

"You said before that you knew what it was like, you knew how hard it could be. So, I guess, um . . . I was just wondering how."

For a while, she didn't think he was going to answer her at all. And then, finally, "I don't like to talk about that stuff."

She'd figured that much out. He never said anything about his past, never talked about what his life had been like before they met at the Center. And sometimes, when she was talking about her memory loss, complaining about what it was like to lose a whole life, he looked almost . . . jealous.

"Sorry," she said quietly. "Is it okay that I asked?"

"No."

"Are you, um, kidding again?"

"No."

J.D. felt like she was going to throw up again, and this time it wasn't because of the smell. "I'm really sorry, I didn't —"

"No, it's okay. It's just . . . it's personal, okay? And it doesn't matter anymore. It was a long time ago."

"I get it," she said, even though she didn't, not really. She'd told him everything. *Everything.* She'd trusted him with all her secrets. *But he's only known me for a few days,* she reminded herself. Those few days were her entire life, but it wasn't the same for him. He had a past, a history, a life filled with people he knew better, people he could trust. All she had was Daniel. "I really do. I'm sorry."

"Don't worry about it," he said, turning over so that his back was to her. "Let's just get some sleep."

But when J.D. closed her eyes, all she saw was her mother.

Not dead, not in a broken heap on the floor, her empty eyes staring up at J.D., accusing, judging, and sentencing all in one unbroken gaze.

Alive.

I made gingerbread cookies — your favorite!

J.D. heard the woman's voice, capable and kind. She felt the woman's arms wrapping her in a tight hug, lifting her off the ground and spinning her through the air. And she remembered — even though she knew it had never happened, she *remembered* — being a little girl, gazing up at her mother with adoration, knowing that everything would be okay. That she was safe. That she was loved.

He had planted the memories in her head. Dr. Styron — Ansel Sykes. He had manipulated her and lied to her, tried to erase the only identity she had left, to convince her that she wasn't J.D., she wasn't the person she knew herself to be. He had toyed with her broken mind, leaving her with no way to tell the difference between her memories and their lies. She might never know what was real. J.D. hated him for that. And she hated *her,* too.

But when she closed her eyes, she didn't see the woman she hated.

She just saw her mother.

So she kept her eyes open. And after a long time of shivering in the dark, trying to ignore the scratching and skittering of creatures behind the walls and the distant shouts and sirens rising from the street, she sat up.

During the day, it was easy to be strong, to move forward. It was only at night, when darkness descended, that she felt helpless.

But she *wasn't,* she reminded herself. She had power. She just had to figure out how to use it. And she had to figure it out before anyone else got hurt.

She stared down at the dim outlines of her hands, wishing there was some button she could press, some set of magic words. And maybe there was — but if so, it was lost behind the gray fog, along with everything else.

Still, she had to try. She set her jacket on the floor in front of her and stared hard at it. *Move,* she thought, feeling ridiculous. *Fly across the room. Go, now. Go!*

Nothing happened.

She stretched her arms out in front of her, aiming them at the jacket, and searched herself for that surge of power, waited for her skin to tingle and burn.

Nothing happened.

How did I do it before? she wondered, trying to remember how it had felt, what she had thought, what she had done. *I was angry,* she realized. Each time it happened. *I was so angry I forgot to be afraid.*

So she stared at the jacket again, trying to muster up an emotion. She thought about Ansel Sykes and what he'd done to her. She thought about her mother. She closed her eyes, squeezed them so tight a field of tiny neon dots swam across the darkness, and she tried to get mad.

Nothing happened.

She opened her eyes, and the jacket was still sitting there, unmoved.

I wasn't imagining it, she thought furiously, and now she was mad — at herself. *I can do it.*

But she couldn't, not that night. Maybe not at all. And after several more tries, she finally had to accept it.

J.D. balled up her coat and lay down again, pressing her cheek against the rough wool. *At least no one saw me,* she thought, imagining the look on Daniel's face if he'd known what she was doing. Imagining his laugh. She would try again, she promised herself as she finally drifted off to sleep. And again and again, as many times as it took. She would find out if she really did have the abilities Ansel Sykes believed in, but she would keep the search to herself. At least until she found some answers.

Daniel wasn't the only one who could keep a secret.

J.D.'s head smacked into the wooden floor. The pain stabbed through her dreams.

"Whuh?" Bleary and confused, J.D. opened her eyes. A stocky shadow loomed over her. She scrambled up, backing away like a crab, but someone grabbed her from behind and pulled her to her feet. A rough hand twisted her arm behind her back, and another slapped against her mouth, muffling her scream. She struggled uselessly. Daniel mumbled in his sleep but didn't wake.

He lay on his side, eyes closed, arms curled around his chest for warmth. Lit up by moonlight, the stocky figure raised its foot. J.D. flinched, and her captor twisted her arm harder, so sharply she could almost feel the muscles tear. She squealed in pain. The heavy boot swung into Daniel's stomach. Hard.

Daniel's eyes shot open. He jumped to his feet, fists up, and advanced on his attacker.

The shadowy figure shook his head slowly. Then he pointed toward J.D. She sighed in relief as the hand came off her mouth, then she gasped. Something pressed against her neck. Something cold and hard. And sharp.

The blade — and she knew it was a blade — dug into her neck, not hard enough to break the skin, but close.

Daniel dropped his fists.

"Let go of her," he said. There was no fear in his voice. He was staring hard at J.D., like he was trying to tell her something, and she got the message.

Stay calm. Stay strong. We'll get out of this.

If it weren't for the knife at her throat, she would have nodded. She understood, and she believed.

"Play nice, and she'll be fine," said the one who'd kicked Daniel. When she spoke, J.D. realized it was a kid.

A girl.

"What do you want?" Daniel asked, and although his voice was still steady, J.D. could see his hands were trembling. "We don't have any money. We don't have anything."

Fly across the room, she thought at the knife at her throat. *Knock into a wall,* she thought at the girl.

Do *something,* she thought furiously at herself, at her supposed dangerous powers. But nothing happened. And the knife was still there. Something tickled her throat. A trickle of blood, she wondered, running down her neck?

"This is our place," the girl said. "And I don't remember inviting you over. That seem like polite behavior to you, Tec?"

"Pretty rude," the voice in J.D.'s ear agreed.

"Fine, we'll get out," Daniel said. "Just let go of her, and we'll leave you alone."

The girl shook her head. She rubbed a hand across her short, spiky hair. "But how do I know you won't do it again?" she said. "Seems like we need to teach you a little lesson about other people's stuff." She gestured toward the door, which had nearly fallen off its hinges when J.D. and Daniel forced their way in. "You break my stuff" — she walked over to J.D.

and rested a hand on her shoulder, never taking her eyes off Daniel — "seems like maybe I should break your stuff."

"I'm nobody's *stuff*," J.D spit out, forgetting about the knife in her anger — at least, until it bore down harder. The grip on her arm tightened. "And this obviously isn't your apartment," she said, now angrier than she was afraid. Up close, the girl looked like she wasn't much older than J.D. She had a pierced tongue and a tattooed chain winding around her neck. And she had long nails, nails that curled around J.D.'s biceps and dug into her skin.

"J.D.," Daniel said warningly, "just —"

"No! They can't just come in here and —" Without warning, she shoved her elbow back. It connected with a stomach, there was a soft *oof* in her ear, and then the grip loosened, just for a second. She ripped her arms free and knocked the knife out of the way. Daniel hurtled across the room and slammed himself into the girl, knocking her down, hard. She slapped at his face, but he grabbed her wrists, pressing them to the floor. A fist grabbed J.D.'s hair and yanked her backward, and she shrieked in pain, whirling around to face her attacker. He was young, too, but big, so much bigger than her, and when she kicked him, he barely flinched, just lunged forward and grabbed her shoulder, pushing her back against the wall.

Then the door flew open. *"Stop!"*

The boy's arms went limp, and he let go of J.D. She backed away — he didn't move. Didn't even look at her. He was just staring at the doorway, his face suddenly looking much younger, and almost scared, like a child waiting for his punishment. Across the room, the girl had stopped fighting Daniel. She, too, was watching the door. A shaft of light filtering through the wooden boards lit up her face. There was no fear, only a soft smile of anticipation.

"Tec, Andi, what's going on here?" the guy in the doorway asked. His voice was rich and deep, almost melodic. And there was something kind about it, J.D. thought. Reassuring. As if now that he was there, nothing else bad could happen.

There was no reason to feel that way. It made no sense — things had probably just gotten significantly worse. Now they were outnumbered. But it didn't feel like that. It felt like they were safe.

J.D. pressed her hand against her throat. There was no blood, no pain. The knife hadn't broken the skin.

"They were trespassing," the girl — Andi —

muttered. "We were just explaining that they had to get out."

"Explaining?" J.D. snorted. "Is that what you call it?"

The guy in the doorway stepped forward into the dim light. He couldn't have been older than seventeen, but the way he stood, his hands in the pockets of his ratty leather jacket, his head tipped to one side, made him look strangely grown up.

"Did they hurt you?" he asked J.D.

"Of course we didn't," Tec said indignantly. "We wouldn't do that."

"I'm asking *her*." He took a few more steps into the room. Tec backed up against the wall.

J.D. rubbed her arm, but she wasn't about to admit that it was sore. "They're just lucky you showed up before *we* hurt *them*."

"We don't want any trouble," Daniel said, crossing the room to join J.D. "We just want to get out of here."

"Get out of here and go where?" the one in charge asked, almost sounding like he actually cared.

"None of your business," J.D. said. She scooped up their coats and took Daniel's arm, pulling him toward the door. "Let's go."

"Wait." The guy stepped into the doorway, blocking their path. He held his hands out to the sides. *No weapons,* the gesture said. *Nothing hidden up my sleeve.* "Tec and Andi just get a little . . . overenthusiastic sometimes. Let us make it up to you." He held out his hand. "I'm Jacob, and I guess you've already met Andi and Tec."

J.D. glared at him. After everything that had happened, she was supposed to just forgive, forget, and make new friends?

After a moment, Jacob let his hand drop.

"So you guys live here?" Daniel asked. J.D. glanced at him, wondering why he was bothering. They could get past this guy, they could get out. There was no reason to stick around and chat.

Daniel still looked wary, but he also looked curious.

Jacob shook his head. "We maintain a number of places for . . . when we need them. Emergencies. Transactions. Anything. It's wise to be prepared." He talked like a grown-up, too, J.D. thought. Like someone used to being in charge. "But most nights we've got a better option. And so do you, now — if you'd like."

J.D. barked out a laugh.

"I'm serious," Jacob said. "Come home with us. It's not a mansion, but anything's better than camping out here, right?"

"Not *anything*," J.D. snapped, though it was hard to stay angry when Jacob's face seemed so open and sincere. "Not getting my throat slit."

"Aw, I wasn't going to hurt you," Tec protested. "Andi just wanted to scare you a little."

"We're fine on our own," Daniel said. He crossed his arms.

Andi started toward the doorway. "See? They're fine. Let's just get out of here."

But she froze when Jacob put his hand on her shoulder. "They're not fine," he said. "They need help."

"We don't need anything," J.D. snapped. In her head, alarm bells were going off. The guy was being nice for no reason. Too nice. "At least not from *you*."

"Oh, really?" He'd stepped out of the moonlight into a patch of shadow, and it was too dark to see his face clearly. But J.D. got the sense he was smiling. "Seems like you could use some food, some blankets, maybe a place to sleep that isn't a rat-infested hole."

"And that's your problem how?"

"It's not." Jacob drummed his fingers against the

65

door frame. "We can leave you here, or you can come with us, get some sleep, get some breakfast. Your call."

"And what's in it for you?" Daniel asked.

Jacob shrugged. "Let's just say I know how it feels to have nowhere to go." Jacob glanced first at Tec, then at Andi. "We all do."

Daniel jerked his head toward the far side of the room, and J.D. followed him into a corner where they could talk privately, keeping their eyes on Jacob and his friends. Tec was whispering something to Jacob, while Andi grabbed his knife and started carving something into the door frame. But Jacob just stared back at them. *Not at us,* J.D. thought, not sure how she could tell, but sure she was right. *At me.*

"I don't trust them," she said softly.

"They've got no reason to lie, but . . . I don't trust them, either." Daniel sighed, and she knew he was thinking about the possibility of sleeping somewhere warm and dry. She was thinking about it, too. "I guess we could stay here, but —"

"But they know we're here," J.D. said. "They could tell someone. If we can't trust them, and we really want to be safe, we probably should find a new spot."

She shivered and rubbed her eyes. She didn't want to go outside again, to wander the streets with her head down against the wind, fighting off sleep, searching — for what? Another empty, mildewed building with rats scuttling across the gritty floors?

They could end up walking the streets all night or curling up beneath a stairwell, too cold to sleep. And sleep was all J.D. wanted. Her body cried for it.

"On the other hand, if we stay with them, we'll know they aren't off ratting on us," Daniel pointed out. "And if they really have blankets . . ."

"And food . . ." J.D. sighed. "It would be really stupid of us to go along, wouldn't it?"

"Probably," Daniel admitted. "But we need somewhere to hide, and Sykes is still out there. We could use some help."

"Strength in numbers, right?"

"It's just one night," Daniel said, giving her a half smile.

"Right. Just one night."

J.D. snuggled deeper into the sleeping bag, sighing with pleasure. The pillow was so soft, the downy fleece wrapped around her so cozy and warm. She could almost forget she was lying in the husk of an old factory, the streetlights filtering through broken windows and gleaming off of abandoned machinery. In the dark, she could barely see the other kids, their sleeping bags sprawled all over the floor, each surrounded by a tiny pile of belongings — torn clothes, soggy books, a one-eared teddy bear, or a rusty knife. There were more than twenty of them, all trying to turn their corner of the factory into something that felt like a home. Daniel lay a few feet away from J.D., already asleep.

Jacob crouched down by her head, bouncing gently on the balls of his feet. "Everything okay? You comfortable?"

She nodded, stretching out in the sleeping bag. "Thanks again for bringing us back here. I still don't get why you did, but thanks."

"I figured you could use a break," he said softly. "After everything you've been through."

Her muscles tensed. "What do you mean?"

"I don't know all the details, of course. I mean, I don't know why you're letting everyone think that you're dead, but —"

She sat up, her heart pounding. "I don't know what you're talking about."

"Come on, J.D.," he said. "I know who you are. I knew it as soon as I saw you. The Girl Without a Past. They know you're alive, you know — I saw it on TV. They've got the whole city out looking for you. There's a reward and everything."

"Please," J.D. said, her throat so tight it came out as a croak. "You can't tell anyone —"

Jacob shook his head. "I understand running away. And I won't say anything, I promise. You're safe here. But, J.D. . . ."

"What?" She steeled herself.

"I don't care what they call you; everyone has a past," Jacob whispered. "And if yours is catching up with you, well . . ." He smiled, but J.D. took no comfort in it. *He knows,* she thought, *he knows who I am,* over and over again, her mind stuttering on the refrain. "If you need someone to talk to," he continued, "I'm here. You can trust me."

She didn't say anything.

"Okay then, sleep well." He bowed his head, stood up, and walked into the darkness.

J.D.'s heart was racing.

"You can trust me," he'd said. But that didn't make her feel any safer.

He won't do anything tonight, she thought, trying to

persuade herself. She wouldn't wake Daniel. He deserved his sleep. And she could handle this herself, keep an eye on Jacob, make sure he didn't turn them in. In the morning, they would decide what to do. For now, J.D. would let Daniel rest.

But she wouldn't sleep. She would lie awake, keeping watch, waiting.

If Jacob did make a move, she would be ready. She would stop him.

Whatever it took.

numbers

"I say we stick around for a while," Daniel mumbled around a mouthful of cold pizza.

"But he *knows*, and I don't trust him," J.D. argued, glancing toward the door where Jacob was hanging with a few of the other kids. They all watched him with that same eager, wary look, J.D. had noticed, keeping their eyes on him, wherever he was in the room. They were always aware of him, of his expression, his mood — and always desperate for his attention. Like puppies waiting for a treat from their master. "What if he turns me in to get the reward?"

Daniel shook his head. "If he'd wanted to turn us in, he could have done it already. What's he waiting for?"

Jacob looked up and caught her eye, like he'd known she was watching all along. One side of his mouth pulled up into a smile. J.D. looked away.

"It's safer here," Daniel pointed out. "It's a good place to hide."

"Until he calls the cops on us."

"The cops aren't our biggest problem," Daniel reminded her. "They can't do anything to us — we haven't done anything wrong. But now that this Sykes knows you're alive and in the city . . ."

"I just don't trust him," J.D. said again.

"All the more reason to stick around and act friendly. If we just stay close and watch him, he won't do anything."

"Then you stay," J.D. offered. "It's safe here for you, and there's food, and all the other kids. I'll just —"

"Disappear?" Daniel shook his head. "I don't think so. I told you already, where you go, I go." He glared at her, as if daring her to argue.

"But —"

"If you don't want to stay here, then *we* leave. Together."

J.D. sighed. "If you really want —"

"This is them," Tec said, popping up behind them.

J.D. slammed her mouth shut. A crowd of kids gathered around her and Daniel.

"Tec told us about you," a girl said shyly, brushing

a strand of limp brown hair out of her face. "We just wanted to say hello. I'm Talia." She blushed, like she was embarrassed by her name, or by speaking at all.

"You're not still mad, are you?" Tec asked. "For, you know, last night?"

"What, you mean that whole thing where you almost killed me?" J.D. asked. "Why would I be mad about that?"

One of the boys gave Tec a shove. "This kid couldn't kill a cockroach," he teased. "Trust me, I've seen him try."

"Shut up," Tec said, shoving back.

The other boy's voice rose to a falsetto. "Oh, gross, a bug! Help me, help me!" Even Tec laughed. "She's the one you've really got to worry about," the kid added, pointing over at Andi. She was sitting with her back against a huge piece of machinery, scratching something into the ground with a long, rusted nail. "Girl's deadly."

"She's not so bad," Talia said quietly. Her voice was soft, and prettier than her face. "She's just, you know . . ."

"Doing what she's gotta do," Tec said. He snatched the last of the pizza crust out of Daniel's hand and tossed it into his mouth. "So talk. Jacob says you guys are okay, but he won't say anything else. What's your story?"

J.D. and Daniel exchanged an awkward look.

"No story," Daniel finally said. "Same old crap, no place to go. No place good, at least."

"So you all, uh, live here?" J.D. asked, skimming over their faces. They looked normal, like every kid she'd passed on the street. Except that their smiles, when they smiled, looked temporary, ready to pack up and go home at a moment's notice. They looked like they could be tough when they needed to be, like the kids at the Center. Like Daniel.

Like me? she wondered.

Tec shrugged. "We live here sometimes. Other times, somewhere else. You know how it is."

No, she didn't. But Daniel nodded.

"Where were you living?" Talia asked. "Before?"

"I . . ." J.D.'s voice trailed off. She couldn't tell the truth, obviously. But for some reason she didn't want to make up a lie.

"We were at the Center for a while," Daniel said quickly. She shot him a grateful smile, but he didn't notice. "But better to go hungry than choke down that meat-loaf surprise, am I right?"

A couple of the kids burst into laughter. "Yeah, I was stuck there a couple years ago. Is that guard still around? Eric? Or Aaron, something like that?" one of them asked. "The one with the giant wart on the side of his neck, with the hair growing out of it?"

"Eric. Yeah, he's still there, and so's the wart. He's always picking at it when he thinks no one's looking," Daniel said. "I saw him once. He pulled the hair right out and then shoved it in his mouth."

"No way!" Tec said, choking back laughter.

"Seriously," Daniel insisted. "I saw him. Guess he got tired of picking his nose."

J.D. smiled, letting the laughter wash over her. No one was looking at her anymore. They were all watching Daniel, who was smiling more than she'd ever seen him. He gestured wildly as he described the Center's cafeteria food, laughing hard, like they weren't on the run, like there was nothing to worry about, like life was good.

They were all laughing, and she didn't know how they could be, especially as they began describing where they'd come from, how they'd ended up sleeping on the floor in an empty factory, hiding out from the cold. Tec's parents were both in jail. The shy girl, Talia, had run away from home the year before. No one ever came looking for her.

There was Pike, who'd lived in twelve foster homes before dropping out of the system. Frick, short for Frederick, whose mother had ditched him at the mall when he was six. Lizzie, who slept in the subways when it was cold and along the river when it was warm. "Until I met Jacob," she said, her pierced tongue just visible through a gap-toothed smile. "Now I sleep here."

Andi drifted over while they were talking, but she didn't say anything about where she'd come from, only that she was never, ever going back.

"What about you?" Talia asked Daniel. J.D. waited for him to scowl and change the subject, as always. But instead he grinned.

"My dad's a thief," he said, sounding proud. J.D. looked at him in surprise, but he wouldn't meet her eyes. "Best cat burglar on the East Coast. When I was a kid, he would use me on his jobs sometimes. Because I was little, you know?"

"Was?" asked Andi, who was several inches taller than Daniel. She looked fierce for a moment, then, unexpectedly, cracked a smile.

"Okay. *Am* kind of . . . short," Daniel admitted,

grinning back. "But back then, I was so small, I could squeeze into crawl spaces, unlock windows for him. Not that he needed me to, usually. My dad's never met a lock he couldn't pick."

So that's where he got it from, J.D. thought. When they first met, Daniel had taught her how to pick a lock, but he'd never said how he'd learned to do it. Or why.

"What'd he steal?" Tec asked, his eyes wide.

Daniel shrugged. "Jewelry, silver, antiques, TVs. We used to travel all over, just blow into these small towns, case out a mansion, do the job, then get out of town before they even knew they'd been hit. Cops never even had a chance."

"So where is he now?" Andi suddenly asked, a sour look on her face. "Super dad? He ditch you when you got too big to slide down a chimney?"

Daniel looked down at his hands. He was fumbling with a paper clip, twisting it and untwisting it, tying it into pretzels. "You always get caught, that's what my dad says. No matter how good you are, no one can be perfect forever. You always make a mistake."

"He got caught?" J.D. asked quietly.

You always *get caught,* she repeated silently to herself. Was it just a matter of time?

"Ten years," Daniel muttered. "But he could be out on parole in seven. And when he is, we're getting out of here, going somewhere warm. Jamaica, maybe. Or Rio. Plenty of sun, plenty of rich people. The good life. It's coming. And in the meantime . . ."

"In the meantime, we're sneaking into *Cape Vampire II* today," Tec said eagerly. "I already saw it twice."

"I saw it three times," Pike boasted.

Tec glared at him. "Anyway, it's awesome. Plus Andi always snags us free popcorn. She's the master, right?"

Andi blushed. She stood up, brushing off the seat of her jeans. "You should come," she muttered, almost too quietly to hear. When she said "you," she wasn't looking at J.D., only Daniel.

"Definitely. Oh." Daniel looked over at J.D. "No. We've kind of got, uh, some stuff we've got to do today."

"What kind of stuff?" Andi asked.

What would she think, J.D. wondered, if she heard the truth? *Stuff like tracking down the crazy scientist who's after me. Stuff like figuring out why some woman pretended to be my mother and then tried to kill me. Stuff like tracking down LysenCorp and finding out whether I'm their property.* Somehow, she didn't think they would all laugh and nod in recognition, giving her a "you're one of us" smile. They would probably stare at her like she was some kind of freak. And maybe they would be right.

There wasn't anything she could do about that. There wasn't any way she could pretend to be normal. Not even for a few hours, not even for a few minutes. But Daniel could. And after everything he'd done for her, maybe she owed him that.

"You should go to the movies," she told him.

"But what about . . . you know. What we were talking about before?"

"It can wait," she said. "For now at least. But" — she bent her head toward him and lowered her voice — "I should probably stay inside, so no one recognizes me. Keep my eye on . . ." She darted her eyes toward the other end of the room, toward Jacob. "Play it safe, right?"

He looked doubtful. "We should do more research."

"We'll do it later," she said. "Actually, I could use some more sleep after last night." *After your new friends here almost killed us.* But she had to admit it to herself: Daniel would be safe with them. J.D. was the one who attracted danger. "So I can just stick around here and relax, and you go to the movies, and we'll do that stuff later. Or tomorrow or something." The lies came so easily. Easier than she would have liked. Daniel was the one person she'd always been truthful with — it should have been hard to lie to him. But it wasn't.

"And you will be here when I get back, right?" he said. "You're not trying to ditch me? Because I told you before —"

"I'm not going anywhere," she said firmly. "Go to the movies. Have fun."

And from the smile on his face when he turned away, she knew he would.

She watched them as they headed toward the door, Daniel at the center of the group, like he'd known them for years. Like he belonged there. They were teasing each other, laughing, happy.

I'm not jealous, she told herself as Daniel slapped Pike on the back and disappeared out the door. *It's good for him to go.*

Just like it was good for her to stay. She didn't need new friends. And despite what she'd told Daniel, she didn't need sleep. She just needed answers.

And today she was going to get them.

This library was much smaller than the last, and there was no special room for the computers. J.D. had to perch on a stool in the middle of a wide-open room, hunching over the screen and trying to ignore everyone around her. *They're not watching me,* she told herself, tugging Tec's old baseball cap down lower on her head. It was the best disguise she'd been able to find. *They don't care.* Still, she couldn't help feeling exposed.

She was tempted to leap off the stool and run out of the building, disappear into the crowded street. But she couldn't. Not if she wanted to continue her search. And she needed to continue.

The building's heat was blasting at full force, and the air was too dry, like all the moisture had burned away. It sat heavy on her lungs, and her clothes weighed her down, heavy and hot. Before she left, Jacob had offered her a change of clothes, but she turned him down, not wanting to accept anything from him. Now she wished she hadn't been so stubborn. She'd been wearing the same thing for days, and the touch of the grimy fabric made her skin crawl.

Sweat beaded on her flushed skin, but she ignored

it, like she ignored everything else. The only thing that mattered now was the computer screen. She wasn't leaving until she found an answer.

She skimmed through article after article on hypnosis and brainwashing, trying to understand what Ansel Sykes had done to her brain. One sentence jumped out at her, repeated in every article she read: *You cannot be hypnotized to do something you wouldn't do when you were awake.* It should have made her feel better — it meant Sykes's control over her had never been complete. But it didn't change the fact that he had lulled her into a relaxed state and implanted thoughts and memories in her mind. He had *invaded* her, and she wouldn't feel safe again — she wouldn't feel *whole* again — until she figured out why.

But after an hour of searching for more information about Ansel Sykes, she still had nothing. Google pulled up several pages about LysenCorp, but nothing useful, nothing about Sykes or his research. She couldn't even find an address for the company.

The article databases were, at first, just as useless and just as frustrating. But then she found her first real clue. It was just a brief notice in a local newspaper, so small that her eyes almost skimmed over it. It wasn't the headline that caught her eye but the photo. The black–and–white picture showed a broad meadow clouded with smoke. A fiery pile of twisted metal smoldered in the foreground. Helicopter Crashes on Private Property, the headline read. Cause of Crash Unknown.

Cause unknown, she thought, holding her breath as she stared at the meadow, at the pile of burning wreckage. *But I know, don't I?*

The black–and–white photo blazed into color and expanded to fill her field of vision. The library faded away, as the tables, the people, the computers turned transparent. J.D. struggled to hold on to them. *This is real,* she told herself. *I'm here, in the present, in the library. Safe.* But tight as she squeezed, it wasn't tight enough, and her grip on the real world slipped away.

She is in the meadow, and it is green and wide and beautiful. The air smells like fresh-cut grass.

She faces them, the man with the cruel eyes and the woman with the crueler smile. When she looks at the woman, the fear makes her insides burn.

"Destroy it," Dr. Sykes says, his voice a low hum that almost seems to come from inside her head. And there is something inside her head, so low she can barely hear it, not a hum, not a buzz, but a melody. It is soft and beautiful; it carries her away from herself. "Destroy it," Dr. Sykes

says again, and the woman smiles. She feels her own lips curl up in response, and she lifts her arms in the air.

A thundering wind hurtles through the meadow, flattens the grass, and the helicopter hovers above them.

Her fear drains away. The music rises, drowns out the thunder of the copter. She is calm. She is trained for this and knows what she has to do.

She focuses, blocking out the wind and the grass and the thunder and the sky. She turns inward, breathes deep, closes her eyes. The images flicker across her mind, what she wants to happen, what she wills to happen. She can almost feel the metal propeller slicing against her hands, can hear the crack it will make when she snaps it in two. It is so clear, so vivid — and then she makes it real.

The heat builds up inside of her, rushing up her body, gathering in her arms, a raging fire. Power. She crackles with energy, with desire. "Destroy it," he said, and she wants to destroy it, needs to release the energy, to take control, and it shoots out of her, like a spark ripping across her body. The propeller snaps, and the helicopter lurches, then plummets.

It screams as it falls, a sharp, thin whistle of desperation. And then the crash, so hard that it shakes the ground, so loud that her ears ring. Are still ringing so loud that she can barely hear the explosion.

Fire. Smoke. Flames. Heat warms her face.

The woman nods at Dr. Sykes. "She's ready."

She doesn't feel ready. She doesn't feel anything. She stands still, her arms at her sides, and waits. They will tell her what to do next.

She stands, and she waits, and she stares into the fire, and she wonders if she hears a scream.

J.D. opened her eyes and the library was back, just as it was.

The heater still rattled, but J.D. felt like an ice cube was slithering down her spine. She took a few deep breaths, trying to push the images out of her head, trying to focus. And then, without knowing why, she closed down the article about the helicopter and ran another search. She found the article almost immediately.

Tragic Fire Claims Girl Without a Past

There it was, right next to the column of text, just as she'd remembered it. A photo of "Laura Collins," the woman who was not her mother. Her blond hair was pulled back into a loose ponytail, and even in the tiny photo, her eyes were bright and warm. She looked like the kind of woman who would bake her daughter gingerbread cookies and brush away her tears. She looked like a mother. *She looks like* my *mother,* J.D. thought, hating herself for it.

She still got flashes of a childhood that never existed, still remembered her mother's cool hand against her forehead. Still longed to snuggle up against her on the couch, watching a movie, falling asleep on her shoulder.

No, she thought with cold anger. *No.* She refused to allow the warm memories to burrow into her. She refused to allow her enemies to have any more power over her. *I hate you,* she thought, staring at the woman in the picture. *I hate you!* And the heat rushed through her on a tide of anger, and though she hadn't touched it, the computer screen flew off the desk, smashing into the floor, but that wasn't enough to calm the anger, which simmered and swelled until it exploded again. Another computer flew off the desk, and another, until she was surrounded by a heap of circuitry and broken glass.

"What are you doing?" someone cried, rushing toward her.

J.D.'s mind was a cloudy swirl of emotion, with no space for thought. Her body was on fire with energy. She couldn't respond, couldn't think, could only act. So she ran, out of the building, down the street, into the crowds, into the cold.

Away.

She ran until she could breathe again. The icy air sliced through her lungs, through the fog of her mind.

I did that, she thought in wonder, in horror. There was no more doubt. *I threw those computers with my mind.*

Just like she'd destroyed the helicopter.

Just like she'd destroyed the woman who was not her mother.

She had power. Unbelievable power. She just had to learn to control it — before someone else got hurt.

attack

Sleep, she told herself, squeezing her eyes shut and trying to relax her muscles. Nightmares or not, it was the only way to escape from herself. She'd spent the day wandering, trying to forget everything she'd found out, if only for a few hours. She had stuck to empty backstreets, knowing it was dangerous to be out in public but unwilling to hide out. After what had happened in the library, she needed to be outside. It was the only way to keep herself from feeling trapped.

But the noises of the city couldn't drown out the sounds of the helicopter crashing into the ground. And the heavy smog just reminded her of the smoke, the smoke that smelled like gasoline, that poured out of the wreckage. The wreckage that she had created.

Was there someone in the helicopter? she kept asking herself, but there was never an answer. Just a half-remembered noise, a thin, high, wavering note that could have been the wind.

Or could have been a scream.

In the vision, it had been so easy. She had closed her eyes, visualized what she wanted to do, then reached inside herself and *done* it. She hadn't been angry or afraid, she had been calm. Focused. In control.

J.D. didn't get it. Because with Mel, with the computers — with her mother — she had felt like she was *losing* control. Like something too big and too powerful lay inside of her, waiting to explode.

There was another way. She knew that now. She just needed to find it.

J.D. had returned to the hideout only when she was too tired and cold to walk any farther. Head down, she had steeled herself to face Daniel. The note she left had explained where she was going, had told him not to worry. But as soon as he saw her, he would want to know what was wrong, and she wasn't ready to talk.

When she walked in, Daniel was surrounded by his new friends and a stack of pizza boxes. He waved a slice at her, but she shook her head and stumbled off into the dark corner where her sleeping bag was pushed up against the wall. Daniel turned back to the group and finished his story.

"Everything okay?" Jacob said as she passed by.

J.D. just nodded, hunched her shoulders, and kept going. He sounded genuinely concerned, and for a second, J.D. was tempted to stop and pour it all out. But she remembered what had happened the last time she had trusted. Dr. Styron had betrayed her. Her mother had betrayed her. Her own memory had betrayed her. The only one she could trust was Daniel, and Daniel was busy.

So she would sleep. For a few hours she would forget. Except that the floor was too hard, too cold, her stomach too empty. And closing her eyes didn't block out the laughter drifting over from across the room. It wasn't fair, she thought.

She should be over there, she should be laughing and joking and eating pizza. She should be normal, like Daniel. But she wasn't.

She had to stay there, a safe distance away, alone. It was best for everyone.

Footsteps.

She lay very still, keeping her breaths slow and even. The footsteps paused, then retreated.

And then they were back again. "I know you're

not sleeping." It was Daniel's voice. She opened her eyes.

He knelt by her sleeping bag, a teasing smile on his face. "Can't fool me," he said. "What's going on?"

"I'm just tired. And if *some* people would just let me get some sleep . . ." The annoyance was just an act. She didn't want him to see how she was really feeling. Grateful that he had come over. Relieved that he still cared.

Daniel lowered himself to the ground and propped his elbows on his knees, resting his chin in his hands so their faces were almost level. "What happened today?" he asked, serious now. "What did you find out?"

She wanted to tell him. But it wasn't fair to keep dragging him deeper into this, to make it his problem, too. Because of her, *he* was on the run. Because of her, *his* life was in danger. Maybe now his life could finally go back to normal — if she let it.

"Nothing big," she said. "Just more of the same. You know."

"I *don't* know," he said. "That's why I'm asking. Don't you trust me enough to tell me?"

"Like you trust me?" she spit out.

He flinched.

J.D.'s fingers flew to her mouth, pressing her lips shut. She hadn't meant to say that. But now it was said, and she was angry enough not to take it back.

"What's that supposed to mean?"

"You know what it means." J.D. turned over on her side, facing the wall.

He grabbed her shoulder and rolled her over onto her back. "Spell it out for me. Since when don't I trust you?"

J.D. sighed and pushed herself up on her elbows. She didn't want to say it out loud. She had no right to be upset about it. But she knew Daniel. He wouldn't let it drop.

"Why did you tell them all that stuff?" she asked quietly. The flare of anger had faded. But she still needed to know. "About your dad, and where you were before the Center? You never want to answer anything I ask you, but then we get here, and it's like you'll tell *them* everything." She looked down, not wanting to see his face. "I mean, it's none of my business," she added quickly. "It's your life, you can talk about it to whoever you want, I just . . . Why wouldn't you tell me?"

Daniel didn't say anything. She sneaked a look at

him. His shoulders were hunched and his hands balled into fists. They banged softly against his crossed knees.

"You want to know about my life?" he asked, his voice still soft but more intense now, almost harsh. "You want to know all the pathetic details? You want to know about my dad coming home drunk every night, when he came home at all? You want to know about being hungry, and dirty, and failing out of school because instead of doing my homework I was staying up all night cleaning up my dad's puke?"

"But what about . . . all that stuff you said? About how he was a thief, and he trained you to break into mansions, and —"

"Oh, he was a thief, all right," Daniel said, looking like he wanted to spit out the taste of the memory. "Just not a very good one. And he didn't rob houses." He laughed once, a broken, angry noise. "Gas stations. That was his thing. Hit the place in the middle of the night, pull out a gun, grab the cash. He used to make me wait in the car. It almost got me killed one time when the guy who worked there came after us with a shotgun. But he didn't care. He was probably sorry he couldn't just get rid of me."

"I don't get it," J.D. said softly. "Why did you make all that other stuff up?"

"Because the truth is pathetic," Daniel said, grinding his nails into the palms of his hand. "You think anyone wants to hear about that? You think I want to *talk* about it? So I made stuff up, something that sounds better. I just . . . I didn't want to lie to you." He curled his hands together and brought them up against his mouth. His shoulders trembled. J.D. rested a hand on his back, but he jerked away.

"What happened to him?" she asked quietly.

Daniel didn't look up. "Jail," he mumbled. "That part was true. Got caught on a security camera one time when he was too drunk to remember a mask. He didn't even go to trial. Just let them send him away."

"For how long?"

"What's the difference? It's not like he's coming back for me. He doesn't even know where I am. He doesn't care."

"And your mom?"

He shrugged. "She ditched us both. So, lucky me, I'm supposed to get bounced through the system until they decide it's time to let me out. Guess I got tired of waiting."

J.D. didn't know what to say. "I'm sorry." It seemed so small, so useless, but it was all she could come up with.

"Don't be." He shook his head. "You didn't do anything."

"I shouldn't have asked. You didn't want to tell me. I should have been okay with that."

"No. I'm —" He took a deep breath and let it out slowly, his eyes closed. Then he finally looked up and met her gaze. His eyes were rimmed with red, but they were dry. "I'm glad you did. I'm glad you know."

She wanted to hug him, or do something, say anything that would make things better. She couldn't fix his past any more than she could fix her own. But she could do something about his present.

"Thank you for telling me," she said.

"Okay. So now you know." He gave himself a violent shake. "Which means it's your turn. Tell me."

J.D. shook her head. She wanted to. The words were scrambling up her throat, forcing their way into her mouth. But she swallowed them, hard. "It's really nothing. I just found a couple more articles about Sykes, but nothing really useful."

"That's it?"

"Yeah. I only looked for, like, an hour. Then I just gave up." She almost didn't want him to believe her. She didn't want him to think she would be like that: weak. A quitter.

His eyes narrowed. "So where were you all day?"

"Around. I just needed to, you know, get away from everything for a while." At least that part was true.

"Yeah." He nodded. "I get that."

"But I'm okay now." She hoped she sounded sincere, even though that was the biggest lie of all. And she hated lying to him. "I just want to go to sleep. You should go back —" She nodded toward the group still hanging out by the pizza boxes and wondered who had paid for them, where they'd gotten the cash. Somehow, she knew that would be the wrong question to ask. "Sounds like you're missing all the fun."

Daniel glanced over at them, and she could tell he wanted to go. "You sure there's nothing you're not telling me?"

"Sure. Promise."

He didn't smile, but something in him relaxed. She could see the tension leak out of him. His neck and shoulders unclenched, and his fingers stopped fussing with the stray threads of denim at the worn cuffs of his jeans. That was enough to tell her she'd done the right thing. "First thing tomorrow morning, we'll figure this thing out," he said. "You and me, together. No more secrets."

"No more secrets," she agreed.

When he was gone, she lay down again and closed her eyes. The laughter was even louder than before, and she could hear Daniel's voice above the rest of them. He sounded happy.

The floor was still hard, the air still cold, her stomach still empty. But this time, she didn't have any trouble falling asleep.

The dream is not a dream.

There are no words; there is no story. There are only images, faces, places flickering through her mind, melting away as she reaches for them. Disappearing into the fog.

And through it all, there is the music.

The same melody, always the same melody. Light and sweet and simple, a fluttering, tinkling melody. A constant.

The meadow morphs into a city street, burned and empty. Then an old barn. A fire.

Her mother's face.

Ansel Sykes.

A white room. A soft glow, a flashing light. Purple, then blue, then green. A white table. A white uniform. A long, thin needle.

Pain.

The music plays, her body sings.

The music plays, the notes swell. It crests, it thunders, it echoes. It is a song she knows, a song she loves and a song she hates, and it hurts. It burns. It is inside of her, burrowing deep, driving her thoughts away, driving herself away. It erases the images, eats away at the faces, a cruel acid, and everything melts away into foul gray smoke. Erased. Until there is only a field of empty, bottomless black, and there is the music.

Darkness. Even ·with her eyes open, darkness was everywhere. Night had fallen. And the music played on.

Shadows shifted, outlines emerged. The boy lying at her feet, curled up, tucked in, an arm flung over the sleeping bag. A peaceful face. A face she knew. But the music made it a stranger.

She was awake and asleep at the same time. She was awake, and the music was the dream, and it played on, a lost memory come to life. And she knew what to do. The music drove her.

The room was still. Quiet. Bodies asleep, innocence dreaming. Heavy steel machinery jutted from the wall above the boy. As she stared at it, the steel began to shudder, began to shake. In her mind, she saw it rip itself away from the wall, saw it fall. She felt the cool steel tear away from the rough plaster.

She focused.

The music played.

She reached for the steel machinery, not with her hand but with her mind, and it was all the same, because she could feel herself grabbing it, could feel her hands wrapping around it. And the heat flowed through her, and with a surge of power and strength, she pulled.

There was a thunderous crack.

The boy slept on as death hurtled toward him, and it whistled and whooshed as it plunged and she smiled as the music surged and crested and —

Daniel!

It wasn't a thought; she wasn't capable of thought. It was a lurch of panic that swept over her, tore her away from the music, broke her from the trance. It was a moment of recognition, deep inside, of who he was and who she was and what was about to happen. It was an action, without thought, without hesitation. And it almost wasn't enough.

She grabbed his arm and yanked him out of the way, just before the heavy piece of machinery crashed to the floor. Dazed from sleep, he clung to her. They both looked up, at the hole in the wall, the plaster that had been ripped away. And then down, at the crushed pillow, the cloud of dust billowing up into the air.

"You saved my life," he gasped.

And she let him think so.

She let them all think so. After the screams and shouts died down, they clustered around, wanting to know what happened. She let Daniel tell everyone how she'd pulled him out of the way just in time, saving him from certain death. She said nothing as they wondered how it could have happened. How could the wall have just given way?

She nodded, agreed that it was an amazing coincidence that she'd woken up, looked up, just in time. She let them pat her on the back, let Daniel thank her again and again.

Only one person didn't congratulate her, didn't thank her. One person stayed away. She felt his gaze resting on her, watching. She didn't want to look, but finally she did, and she hadn't imagined it. Jacob was staring, his eyes dark and hooded. Impenetrable. He tapped his finger against his lips and nodded, twice.

But when he finally came over to her, after everyone else had drifted away, he just patted her on the shoulder. "Remarkable," he said quietly. "A real live superhero in our midst."

She forced herself not to recoil from the touch.

And when everyone dragged their sleeping bags across the room, safe from falling machinery, she followed them. When they went back to bed, she let them believe she would, too. But she couldn't afford to sleep. What if it happened again?

I'm dangerous, she thought, staring at the broken machinery, the long, thick rod of steel pinning down Daniel's pillow. She imagined his head still lying there, crushed beneath the steel. She imagined the blood and the dead stare in his eyes. It was too easy to imagine. *I'm out of control.*

There was something inside of her, something that wanted her to lash out, to destroy, to kill.

The music — she could still hear it echoing in her

brain. Ansel Sykes had put it in there somehow. It was a piece of her past. She knew that much. When she heard it, she felt like she was outside of herself, watching what happened, unable to change it, unable to do anything but follow orders. Unable to do anything but destroy. Just like she always felt in the visions and dreams, with Sykes by her side, urging her on. And the melody was always the same.

But in the dreams, she was under his control completely. There was no breaking free. And every time she heard the music, its hold on her got stronger. This time she had snapped out of it. But it had been close.

Too close.

She was strong, but it was stronger. It would be until she found out what it was, found out how to control it. She couldn't risk letting it escape again. She couldn't let anything happen to Daniel. He was the only person in the world who made her feel safe; he was the only person on her side.

But he wasn't safe with her. He wasn't safe *from* her.

And no matter how much she wanted to stay, no matter how much she liked the sound of the word "together" — it gave her strength, it gave her hope — she couldn't. She had told Daniel, over and over again, that he didn't owe her anything. It was true. But she owed him.

She owed him enough to leave him behind.

alone

J.D. slipped out of the building just before dawn. She tiptoed around Jacob, who slept sprawled in front of the entrance, guarding his flock. The door squeaked as she slid it open, and Jacob shifted in his sleep. She froze. He turned over, his eyelids flickering, and then he was still. She shut the door behind her and took a deep breath. This was it; she was leaving.

She hated to go without saying good-bye, but she knew Daniel would never let her leave without him. She just hoped that when he woke up and found himself alone, he would understand.

The city felt empty. Every few minutes, a truck wheezed by and broke the silence, but that was it. She plodded down the sidewalk, choosing a direction at random. It didn't matter, as long as it was away. The more space between her and Daniel, the better. The faster she went, the farther she went, the harder it would be to turn back.

Every block looked the same. Gated storefronts, crumpled wrappers blowing through the gutters, stained sidewalks, the stench wafting up from the garbage-bag mountains lining the curb. The rising sun cast everything in a warm pink glow, but it would take more than mood lighting to soften this side of the city. Even pink and glowing, the world looked grimy and broken.

Now what? J.D. thought as the minutes slipped by, piling into hours. But there was no answer, so she kept walking, hunger gnawing away at her. She had no money, no grand plan, nowhere to go, no one to —

She cut herself off. So she was on her own again — so what? She didn't need Daniel. She didn't need anyone. Hadn't she already proved that she could survive on her own? She had woken up on the street without a memory, without a past, and she had survived. She had made it through the hospital, made it through the Center, made it through the lies and manipulations of Ansel Sykes and her so-called mother, and she had survived it all. She was strong. She could do this.

But do what? LysenCorp was the key to every-thing, she was sure of it, but she couldn't just march into their headquarters and demand answers, demand to know what they'd done to her. She couldn't even figure out where the headquarters were.

Ansel Sykes had disappeared, too. And, after what had happened at the library, she didn't want to do any more research, not in public, not until she was sure she could control herself.

The morning bloomed, and she finally found her way out of the warehouse district. The city came to life with shoppers and strollers and hordes of swanky suits pushing past on their way to Somewhere Important. J.D. barely noticed any of them. She walked with her head down, staring at her sneakers scuffing the pavement. They were silver gray, with swooshes of pink flaring along the sides. They weren't the sneakers she'd been wearing when she was first found at the explosion site. Those were ruined, caked with ash and rubble. But in Alexa Collins's closet, she'd found two neat rows of shoes, pair after pair — black patent leather with pink lin-ing, pink ballet flats, brown all-weather boots with pink lining, pink rubber rain boots, flowery flip-flops with pink wedge heels. Alexa Collins had been very fond of pink.

Alexa Collins was a fictional character, J.D. reminded herself.

A fictional character with very bad taste in clothes. The sneakers had been the only acceptable pair, and they had fit J.D. perfectly.

"Of course they do," her mother had said. "They're yours, honey." Her lip had wobbled like it did whenever J.D. made it sound like Alexa was a different person, someone from the past who was never coming back. Her lip wobbled, and her teeth bit down, holding it steady, making it seem like she was trying to be strong for the sake of her fragile daughter.

She was probably just trying not to laugh.

J.D. rounded a corner, and something — maybe the sound of the girl's laugh, maybe her voice as she called to her friend — made her look up.

There were three of them walking out of the park, all around J.D.'s age. The one in the middle had her arms around the other girls' shoulders. She was shorter than the other two, and light enough that she could rest her weight on them and swing her legs into the air. They yelled at her, but J.D. could tell by their smiles that they liked it. Two had blond hair, not ragged and wispy like J.D.'s but long and thick, with identical platinum streaks. The third was a redhead. Her wild curls blew in the wind.

J.D. smiled at the girls as they passed, without even meaning to. It was accidental, a nod and a shy grin, like she knew them, because, just for a moment, when their eyes met, she felt like she did. *I could have been you,* she thought. *In another life.*

The laughter on their face vanished, and they glared, then tucked their heads down and sped forward.

"Did you see that?" J.D. heard one of them say loudly. "The freak was, like, *staring* at us."

"She probably just wanted some money," another of them said, her voice kinder.

"She doesn't need cash, she needs *clothes*," the first one argued. "Did you see what she was wearing?"

They burst into laughter, and it sounded just as melodically gleeful as the laughter that had first caught J.D.'s attention. She stopped short in the middle of the sidewalk, then stumbled as someone slammed into her from behind. "Sorry," she mumbled, inching toward the edge of the sidewalk, toward a wall that could hold her up. She just wished she could sink into the brick and disappear.

J.D. squeezed her eyes shut tight, willing away the tears. She wouldn't let them make her cry. Not after what she'd been through. Those girls would never have to face the things she'd faced — and if they ever did, they would crumble. Not like J.D., who stood strong, who moved forward. Who didn't cry just because someone laughed in her face.

Her face . . . She caught sight of her reflection in the nearest store window. A smear of dirt ran from her left cheek to her chin. Her hair was tangled and stiff, her eyes were dull and lifeless, rimmed by deep black shadows. No wonder they had laughed. J.D. wasn't one of them — she could see that for herself. She was a freak, like they'd said. She was a creature that had crawled out of the gutter, like a pigeon, like a soggy stray cat, dirty and smelly and liable to bite. Of course they'd laughed. If J.D. was in their place, she probably would have laughed, too. She might even have screamed.

She turned away from the window, back out to the crowd. It seemed like they were all staring at her.

She couldn't breathe.

There were too many of them, too many eyes

cutting through her skin, and she needed to get away. Needed to *hide* away, fade into the darkness so that no one could see her and what she'd become.

There was a multiplex across the street. *It's the best place to hide out from the cold,* Daniel's voice reminded her. J.D. took one last look at her reflection and tried to rub the grime off her face with her palm. But the smear of dirt just spread. *I can't do this,* she thought, struggling to stay calm. *I just need . . .*

But she didn't know what she needed, that was the problem. She didn't know what to do next or where to go, or how to take care of herself.

She needed a break.

The movie theater lobby was warm and crowded, and the old man clipping tickets was barely glancing at the people streaming by. It was easy for J.D. to melt into the crowd, hovering behind a group of teenagers who shoved a fistful of tickets at the old man. They barreled past him before his clumsy fingers could sort through and count the tickets, and J.D. followed. She chose the theater blindly, and when she stepped inside, she didn't even look at the screen. Instead, she just slipped into the second-to-last row and curled up in the plush seat. It felt so good to sit down. It felt so good to fade into the darkness. She closed her eyes.

She slept.

Her eyes opened as the music swelled. Credits rolled as a couple shared a long kiss, their faces huge and bright on the screen, their lives as smooth and flawless as their skin. A few rows in front of J.D., two heads bent together, their lips touching. She wanted to close her eyes again.

But instead, she sidled down to the end of the aisle, where two broken seats hung down so low their cushions brushed the floor. J.D. climbed over them and curled up into a tight ball, sandwiched between the wall and the scratchy seat cushions, hidden from sight. The lights came on, the audience flowed out, and no one saw her. The ushers swept through, mopping spills, grabbing candy bar wrappers, complaining, and still no one saw her. And then the lights flickered out again, and the projector whirred, and J.D. found another seat, and for another two hours she could ignore everything and pretend she was someone else.

The movie, which played over and over again, was filled with sunlight, a desert epic suffused with golden light. So when she finally left the theater, her limbs stiff, her back sore, her mind fuzzy, she expected the sun. But it was long gone, and the only light left was fluorescent.

I wasted a whole day, she thought in horror. Inside the theater, warm and relaxed in her seat, it had been so easy to let the images wash over her. She could lose herself in scene after scene of beautiful people storming through their overdramatic lives. There was no thinking required, only watching and listening, and sometimes not even that, when she let herself drift into sleep. A peaceful, dreamless sleep, with no haunting music. Even in her sleep, she heard the dim crashes and explosions from a screen that was too distant to matter. The noise kept the nightmares away.

But now she was back in the real world, and she was disgusted with herself. *Break time is over,* she thought firmly. She needed to find a place of her own, a home base to sleep and think and plan her next step. She wouldn't waste another day just sitting around and waiting for something to happen. No more hiding away from her problems or her enemies. No more trying to forget. She'd forgotten enough.

It was starting to rain, and J.D. realized she didn't know where she was. She tried to remember which streets she'd taken to get there, but in the dark, nothing looked familiar. The icy rain trickled down her face like tears. She picked a direction at random and started to walk, putting one step in front of the other, ignoring the cold wind and the numbness creeping through her toes. Just one step, then another, and another. Eventually, she would find her way back to the neighborhood Daniel had showed her, the one with the empty buildings and the dirty apartments, their windows boarded up and their doors hanging off the hinges. And if she didn't, she could sleep in an alley. Or in a train station, or . . . somewhere. There was always somewhere, she thought. Always some way to get by.

Survival, J.D. thought. *Making it through one night, then another.* That had to be the beginning, problem number one. And when she'd solved it, she could start on her other problems. She promised herself: Life wouldn't always be about surviving, about just *getting by.* But tonight it was.

Finally, she found the perfect spot. It wasn't the building she'd broken into with Daniel but one that looked just like it, crumbling and boarded up. But before she could congratulate herself and before she could start searching for a way in, she spotted the cop. J.D. ducked behind a parked car.

"You sure you haven't seen her?" the cop asked a man huddling in the doorway. "We have reason to believe she's hanging around this neighborhood somewhere."

The man smiled. He had only four teeth, jagged, crooked splashes of white across a field of black. He shook his head.

The cop shoved a folded-up newspaper in his face. "If you spot her —"

"Yeah. Whatever." The man waved the paper away, and a moment later, the cop headed off down the street.

J.D. huddled behind the car, waiting impatiently for the man in the doorway to leave, too. She couldn't know whether she was the one the cops were looking for, but she couldn't risk it. She had to get away before anyone spotted her.

Finally, the coast was clear, and J.D. darted out from behind the car and began hurrying down the street.

"Hey! Hey, you!" It was another cop, coming from the opposite direction. Coming toward her. And he'd seen her face. "It's her," he told his partner, who'd appeared behind J.D. "J.D., we've been looking for you!"

J.D. ran.

They know my name, she thought as she ran. *Not Alexa. My name. J.D.*

That hadn't been in the newspaper article. Someone had turned her in. Someone she knew.

She ran faster. They stormed after her, splashing through the rain, and she ran faster, skidding on the wet pavement, her hair plastered against her face. Blinded by the water dripping into her eyes, she veered around a corner, down one street and then another. She was losing them — but they weren't giving up. She could hear their voices, distant now, but angry. "Stop! We're not trying to hurt you, we just want to —" The wind in her ears drowned out the rest, and she pushed harder, lungs screaming. She slipped, almost fell, caught herself, ducked into an alley.

Dead end.

A high fence bordered the opposite end, thick barbed wire curling across the top. To her right were two giant garbage bins lodged against a brick wall, and next to them, a door. A locked door.

"No!" J.D. cried, twisting the knob. "Let me in!"

She pounded on the door, then stepped back and threw herself at it, slamming her shoulder into the metal as hard as she could. Pain shot through her arm, but the door didn't open. It didn't even tremble. Then, suddenly, she stopped. Stopped screaming, stopped pounding, just stopped. "I can do this," she said quietly, staring at the door. She put her hand on the knob, closed her eyes, and concentrated on how much she wanted to be inside, how much she needed to be inside, away, *safe*. She dug into herself and scooped out all her anger and frustration, channeled it into her hand, into the knob, into the door . . . and twisted.

Nothing happened.

Another moment, and nothing happened. She could hear the cops drawing closer. If she backtracked, they would spot her, they would catch her. But if she stayed here, it was only a matter of time.

A wave of panic tugged her under, but she broke through. The anger kept her mind clear. Anger at the cops, anger at whoever had sent them, at whoever was after her, anger at herself, at her useless so-called powers, at the knob, at the door, the door that wouldn't open, the door that had to open, the door, the door, the door.

The door.

Something in her mind shifted, settled into place, and the heat rushed through her. Not a blaze this time, but a searing pain, a warm current that welled up from deep inside — and the lock snapped as the door swung open.

She threw herself inside, slammed the door shut behind her.

The lock was broken; there was nothing to stop the cops from bursting through. She stumbled around in the shadows, bumping against something solid and heavy. It was rectangular and waist-high, like a desk, and if she threw all her weight against it, she could just manage to slide it across the floor.

She pushed. And inch by inch, it slid. Too slow.

She could hear the cops' muffled shouting as they barged into the alley, then a crashing, clanging noise.

They're searching the trash bins, she thought, and pushed harder against the heavy piece of furniture, moving it steadily, until it blocked the door. Just in time.

The door rattled, again and again. "Locked," one of the cops said, and the voice sounded like it was only inches away. J.D. stayed very still and very quiet.

"She must've gone over the fence," the other voice

said. "That alley feeds out to Lamont. Come on, let's go!" And then the footsteps pounded again, heading farther and farther away, until there was only silence.

It was pitch-black inside the building, too dark to figure out what it was, or who she might be sharing it with. But it felt empty. It was dry and almost warm and a yeasty smell hung heavy in the air. Wherever she was, she was safe — at least for now. She couldn't go back outside. Not while they were looking for her.

She would stay the night, she decided. And she would stay awake, stand guard, just in case.

J.D. leaned back against the door and hugged her arms to her chest. Someone had told the cops she was out there. Someone had told them where to look. But who?

It couldn't be Ansel Sykes. He wouldn't use the police, she was sure of that. He would have come himself. And he wouldn't have let her get away so easily.

Jacob.

J.D. bit down on her lip sharply, punishing herself for being so stupid.

I know who you are, he'd said.

You can trust me, he'd said.

There was a reward on her head, and Jacob had no reason to protect her. No reason not to turn her in and get the cash. She knew that, and yet she had let herself ignore the threat. Stupid.

She had to come up with a plan. If the police could find her, so could Sykes. The thought of being back under his control sent a sharp pain of terror slicing through her. She just wanted to run again, faster this time, until she was so far away he couldn't reach her.

But she couldn't go anywhere, not tonight. Not while the locked door was all she had to protect herself.

I'll figure something out, she thought with determination. *I'll find out how to control myself, my . . . abilities. And then I'll find Sykes. And I'll stop him.*

Easy to say. But maybe impossible to do. And it was so hard to focus with the cold creeping up into her toes and the fatigue seeping through her muscles. *Stay awake,* she told herself. *Just stay awake.*

But maybe that was just one more impossibility. Because the night stretched on, slow and silent, and soon her head toppled forward and her eyes slid shut.

She stands on the sidewalk as the city swirls around her. Everything is dull and gray, except for the car. It is black, but somehow it shines more brightly than the world around it. It glows.

The long car glides by. The world moves in slow motion. She doesn't move at all. A window rolls down. There is a man inside, and his head turns, so slowly. She sees his face.

The car stops. The world stops. Everything freezes and everything fades, until there is only his face. His green eyes. His narrow gray eyebrows. His brown birthmark, crawling down his forehead, spilling onto his left cheek. His narrow nose, his pale lips. Lips pulled back into a smile.

She feels her lips stretch in response.

The world jolts into motion, the colors seep back in, the car sails on. The man turns away.

This is the moment she has been waiting for. She is well-trained; she is prepared. And now she knows what to do. She sees it unfold in her mind, and she wills the image to become reality, and she reaches toward the long black car as if it is speeding toward her and she is pushing it away.

And the car lurches to the right, as if thrown, flying toward the sidewalk, toward the gas station on the corner. She can still see the man's face. He is still smiling as the car *plows into the pumps. He is still smiling amid the screams.*

And then there is a ball of flame, and she can't see him anymore.

But her own smile is still in place.

enemies

"It's a kid!"

She opened her eyes. A ring of men stood over her. Large men. Large men in baggy jeans and T-shirts, with tattoos and muscles and uniform scowls.

"I'm sorry," J.D. said, scrabbling backward. She slid up into a standing position. Someone had moved the heavy desk away from the door, and she took a step backward, then another, reaching for the knob. "I just needed a place to sleep, I didn't mean to —"

"How'd you get in here, kid?" One of the men stepped toward her, swung his arm up. She jerked away. But there was no contact. Only a dull crack as his hand slapped against the door, holding it shut. "Where's your folks?"

Good question.

"They're . . . I have to go now," she said quickly. "They're waiting for me."

Another of the men laughed. "I doubt that. Nice try, though."

"We should call someone," the first guy said.

"No!" J.D. yelped. "I mean, I don't want to cause any trouble, just let me get out of your way. Please."

"It's none of our business," a third guy said, tugging at his bushy beard. "If she wants out . . ."

There was a long pause, and then the one holding the door shut pulled his hand away and swept his arm out in an exaggerated "after you" gesture.

J.D. sighed as the relief rushed through her. "Thank you. Thanks so much. I won't come back, I promise." She twisted the knob and pulled open the door, flinching at the bitter gust of wind. She took a step toward freedom — and the world lurched. Her fingers grabbed for the door frame, squeezing tight. For a moment, everything righted itself again, was still and level. And then the ground rippled and tipped, tossing her backward, and she stumbled. A hand caught her back before she could drop to the floor. She opened her mouth, wanting to say thank you, but her tongue suddenly felt large and clumsy, her lips numb, her words very far away. Too far to reach.

And the world dimmed, turned gray.

And the wind roared, a thunder that shook her brain.

And her fingers were numb, and everything was numb.

And the light faded away.

And she was gone.

"Slowly," someone said as she squinted into the light and tried to raise her head. "Take it easy."

"What happened?" For a moment, J.D. thought she must have dreamed the whole thing. Because here she was again, lying on the floor, surrounded by the ring of large men. But this time, they weren't scowling. This time, they looked terrified.

"You passed out," one of them said. "One second okay, then the next . . . *splat*."

"How long's it been since you had anything to eat?" asked the man with the fuzzy black beard.

At the thought of food, J.D.'s stomach knotted, and another wave of dizziness swept over her. "A long time, I guess." She struggled to sit up. "I have to get out of here." But the world still wobbled when she moved.

"You're not going anywhere," the first man said.

He had sandy brown hair and a misshapen left ear, like someone had taken a bite out of the top. "Not till you get something to eat." He jerked his head toward one of the others. "Mike, grab the —"

"Yeah, on it."

They guided her into a folding chair. Someone pulled out a thermos, and someone else handed her a cardboard box that smelled so sweet and fresh. . . . "Ohhh," she gasped in pleasure, flipping open the lid. Cracked sugar glaze layering sweet, soft, round cake, and buried in there beneath the sprinkles and the powdered sugar, was that — ?

"A chocolate doughnut." She sighed, taking a slow bite and savoring the rich sweetness. "Mmm . . ." She washed it down with a swig of steaming-hot coffee. The men — Mike, Randy, Juan, and Carl with the ragged ear — stared at her as she stuffed her face, laughing at the chocolate glaze smeared across her chin. And once they were laughing, they weren't so scary anymore.

She'd stumbled through the back door of a pretzel factory, they told her, which explained the smell.

They were on the early shift, charged with readying the machines before the other workers arrived. They didn't ask her how she'd gotten in, or why she was there, or anything else. None of them talked much at first, except for the one named Randy, who launched into a ten-minute joke but shut up just before the punch line when Juan elbowed him in the gut. "She's just a kid," Juan whispered, and Randy turned bright red and didn't say anything more.

Carl, who seemed to be in charge, didn't speak at all. As J.D. started on her second doughnut, he got up from the table to go start up the machines on the main factory floor. Once he was gone, the other men opened up, talking about cars and movies and complaining to her about their boss, who — lucky for J.D., they said — was out for the week. They talked about pretzels and how it was impossible to eat them after working in the factory for more than a week. They talked about their wives and their kids and who had dropped the ball in that weekend's touch football game. And then, just when J.D. had started her third doughnut, beginning to relax, they talked about her.

"So . . . you run away from home or something?" Juan finally asked.

J.D. shook her head.

She wasn't lying. Home was what she was running *to*. She just didn't know where to find it.

"She's a runaway, all right." It was Carl. He was back, and he wasn't alone.

J.D. leaped out of the chair, but Juan grabbed her wrist and squeezed tight. Not tight enough to hurt her.

But tight enough.

"Sorry, kid," Carl said, tugging at his ear. "But there's that reward, and —"

"Yeah, I get it," J.D. muttered. "You don't owe me anything." No one did.

"Let's go now," said the cop standing to Carl's left. He shook his head. "They've got everyone out looking for you, and *I'm* the one who finds you?" He smiled and, before J.D. could react, jerked her arms behind her, slapping her wrists into a pair of metal cuffs.

"Whoa!" Carl said. "Is that really necessary? She's just a kid!"

"Standard procedure," the cop told him, locking his grip on J.D.'s shoulders. "For this one, at least. I've got orders." She tried to squirm away, but his hold was firm. The metal cuffs bit into her wrists. "For her own good, just until we can get her down to the station and deal with her."

I can stop this, she thought. *I can stop this now.*

But could she? Even with her hands locked behind her back?

He's just doing his job, she told herself. And the men were just trying to help. Even Carl. She couldn't blame him for wanting the reward. She couldn't blame any of them. *But I could stop them,* she thought. Her uncertainty faded away, and suddenly she was pretty sure she could. *I could* hurt *them.*

And part of her wanted to. Part of her wanted to very much.

Which was why she let the cop push her out the door. She let him think he was in charge, guiding her to the patrol car, opening the door, then, with a heavy hand on her head, forcing her into the backseat.

The cop flicked on his radio. "This is unit three five seven. I got the girl," he reported to his dispatcher. "Bringing her in now."

The car was cold and it smelled like something was rotting under the scratched leather seat. Her hands still cuffed, J.D. couldn't hold on as the cop tore through the streets. His sharp turns tossed her back and forth across the seat, slamming her first into the door, then flinging her in the other direction. She tipped over, her head thudding into the seat, and she stayed in that position, her cheek against the leather. She shut her eyes, listened to the motor rumble and the windshield wipers squeak.

"What's going to happen?" she asked the cop when he let her out of the car and pulled her toward the station. "What will they do with me?"

He didn't answer. Didn't even look at her. She would think he'd forgotten she was there, if not for the fact that his fingers still dug into her arm. He jerked her up the steps.

"Who sent you after me?" she asked, refusing to give up. "Who told you I was out there?"

No answer to that one, either.

But it turned out she didn't need him to tell her. Because as he pushed her through the station doors, she got her answer. Her answer was sitting across the room, slouched in a black metal chair. Her answer stood up when she walked in, his eyes bright and hopeful, his expression a mixture of guilt and relief.

She saw him, and she knew her betrayer. The one who'd told the cops where to look for her, who'd sent them on the hunt. The one responsible.

She'd tried to protect herself, she'd tried not to let

anyone else in, knowing that no one could be trusted, knowing that, in the end, anyone could betray her. But she hadn't protected herself enough, had she? Because this was the one answer she hadn't expected, the one betrayal she had thought — *known* — to be impossible.

This was Daniel.

"You can wait here with your friend," the cop told J.D., shoving them both into a small waiting room. "At least till they're ready for you." He unlocked the cuffs, and J.D. resisted the temptation to rub her wrists. She didn't want him to know how much they hurt.

"He's not my friend." She couldn't even look at him. At Daniel.

The cop didn't respond. He just turned his back on them and walked out. She heard the lock turn.

Trapped, she thought. Even if she could distract the guard sitting in the corner, watching her, even if she could break through the locked door — and she thought maybe she could — there was a whole station full of cops on the other side. She was trapped.

Daniel was trying to get her attention. J.D. kept her eyes fixed on the cop sitting across from her. She stared at his black loafers, his crisply pressed navy pants. Mostly, she stared at his gun. It sat in a holster, resting just above his hip. It was the first time she'd seen a real gun up close. She ran her eyes along the dull black metal, the smooth curve of the trigger, the long, thick barrel that disappeared into the leather holster. The man's hand rested at his waist, his fingers grazing the metal grip. His nails were crusted with dirt, and a hangnail on his thumb had started to bleed. He tapped the grip lightly, as if making sure that the gun was still there. In case he needed it.

"J.D., will you just look at me? I'm sorry."

She forced herself not to react. *The gun,* she told herself. *Focus on the gun.* Because the gun was a reminder of where she was and what she faced. It was a reminder of what Daniel had done. "Sorry" wouldn't fix that.

"I didn't know it would go down like this. I'm *sorry.*"

"Sorry for what?" she snapped, no longer able to stay silent. "Sorry you'll have to split the reward?"

"You know it's not about that! You disappeared, and I thought — I thought Sykes got you. I didn't know what else to do!"

She didn't speak.

Daniel sighed. "I panicked, okay? I was just trying to help. And maybe now, maybe it'll be okay?"

Yeah, right. Okay. She stared at the gun.

"Look." He slid his chair closer to hers, earning a sharp look from the guard. Daniel lowered his voice to a whisper. "I can fix this. We can get out of here. We just need to distract this guy, and then —"

"No. *We're* not doing anything." J.D. finally looked up at him. And something inside her broke.

All this time, all these days of fear and uncertainty, she'd calmed herself with a single thought: *Daniel.*

Daniel will help.

Daniel will know what to do.

Daniel will believe me.

Daniel will listen.

It had been her security blanket, her talisman, her last candle in the darkness. And now he'd blown out the light.

The day before, wandering the streets, hiding in the movie theater, running from the cops, she'd thought, *I have no one.* But that had been a lie, because in the back of her mind, she'd known that she still had Daniel. That she could always go back.

This time, there was no lie. This time, Daniel had

shown her the truth about himself, the truth about what his promises were worth. Nothing.

The door swung open.

"All right, time for you to go," a woman said brusquely, marching over to Daniel and pulling him out of the chair. "You're lucky the Chester Center's willing to take you back again."

Daniel winced, and J.D. tried not to feel a stab of sympathy. She knew that for Daniel, "lucky" wasn't the word for it. "Lucky" had been escaping from the Center, finding a new place to live, a place with other kids and cold pizza and freedom. "Lucky" would have been disappearing and never seeing the Center again.

"What about J.D.?" Daniel asked, jerking his arm away from the cop.

"Oh, she's not going back there," the cop said.

And the tiny kernel of sympathy disappeared.

"There's some people who've been looking pretty hard for this one," she continued. "And I'm sure they'll be *very* appreciative for your help."

Daniel's jaw dropped. J.D. could see the under-standing in his eyes. It was *them*. Sykes. LysenCorp. They had found her. Because of Daniel, they had found her.

"I'm so sorry," he pleaded, flailing uselessly as the cop dragged him out of the room. "I didn't know this would happen!"

"But it did," J.D. said softly, too softly for him to hear. And then Daniel was gone, and the door clicked shut again, and she was left alone with her fear, and her bitterness, and the gun.

Too much of anything could get boring after a while. Even terror.

So after an hour, J.D. started looking for something else to fill the time, something aside from running through nightmare scenarios in her head, imagining what Ansel Sykes and LysenCorp would do to her when they got her back. The cops had left a stack of magazines for her to read, and even though they all looked hideously dull, they were better than nothing. She began leafing through the one on top, flipping quickly through long, boring articles on foreign policy and international economic summits. *Better to stare blankly at the wall,* she thought, and was about to close the magazine again when she caught sight of the picture.

She recognized him from the birthmark. The green eyes could have belonged to someone else. The long, sharp nose could have been anyone's. The gray hair, the narrow eyebrows, the faint, cryptic smile playing on his lips, it was all familiar, but not familiar enough. It wouldn't have been enough to make her squeeze the magazine until her fingertips faded white, to make her lungs seize and her face pale. It wouldn't have been enough to make her tremble with recognition, with confusion, with horrified guilt.

It wouldn't have been enough — but the birthmark was. The brown birthmark cresting over his forehead, the birthmark of the man in her dream. The man whose limousine she sent flying into a gasoline pump, a man she'd last seen exploding into a ball of fire.

Goran Czernick, the popular Strovenian reformer, will spend one week in the United States, meeting with prominent political and economic figures in an attempt to rally American support for his country's reforms. His visit is timed to coincide with an international summit at the end of the month, at which Czernick will deliver the keynote address to the assembled world leaders. Czernick has vowed to do whatever it takes to reinstate democracy in

Strovenia before the end of the decade, and sources predict that his movement may accomplish the goal even sooner than expected.

J.D. had never heard of Strovenia or Goran Czernick, but she was certain she knew him. She would never forget that face or the sound of his screams, and here was proof that he wasn't just a figure conjured up in her dreams. He was real. Just like her nightmare vision of the helicopter crash had been real. The article she'd found on the computer had confirmed it. And this dream had seemed just as vivid, just as intense — and now here was evidence that the man, Goran Czernick, was real.

But he was also alive. The magazine was only a few days old, and according to the article, Czernick wasn't arriving in the country for another week. So J.D. couldn't have killed him, no matter how real the vision had felt. She stared at his picture, assuring herself that he was alive, that he was safe, but the guilt still gnawed at her. She had seen his face. She had flicked her hand. She had heard his screams.

It felt real, but so did the memories of her childhood, the fake ones that Ansel Sykes had implanted in her brain. Could he have implanted this one, too? But why?

An idea popped into her head. She didn't want to believe it, didn't even want to think about it, but once it was there, she couldn't shake it away.

What if it wasn't a memory of something she had done?

What if it was a vision of something she was supposed to do? Something she'd been *programmed* to do?

Just like the music, she thought. *Just like the dreams, when I have no control over myself — when I do exactly what* he *says.*

What if Ansel Sykes had found a way to control her telekinetic abilities, and what if this was what he intended her to do with them? She knew what he wanted from her — he'd said it himself. He wanted her to *destroy*.

What if Goran Czernick was the one she was supposed to destroy next?

It didn't seem possible. No one could force her to blow up that car. No matter what they did to her, no matter what kind of control they had, no one could force her to kill. She suddenly remembered what she had learned about hypnosis: *You cannot be hypnotized to do something you wouldn't do when you were awake.* Ansel Sykes couldn't force her to destroy. He couldn't turn her into a killer — not unless, deep down, she was one already.

But aren't you? she thought, remembering her mother falling to the ground. *No one was controlling you then.*

Frustration welled up in her, so strong and sudden that it overpowered the fear. If only she could just remember who she was, where she had come from, how she ended up at the explosion site, *something . . .* anything.

But there was nothing. The wall keeping her from her past was too tall, too wide, too slippery. It crumbled only in her nightmares, and even then, it was only enough to remind her how much she didn't know and how defenseless she was in her ignorance. She slumped down in the chair, leaning her head back against the wall.

The doors flew open, and light streamed into the dim room. Two men, dark, trim silhouettes, appeared on the threshold. They strode forward in unison, their shoes slamming the tile with rhythmic cracks, and stopped in front of the guard in the corner. Their black suits seemed to suck in the light; their eyes hid behind dark glasses. The badges they flashed were gold, and when they slipped them into their pockets, their jackets slid back, revealing their holsters.

J.D. sat up straight. They weren't facing her, hadn't looked in her direction at all since stepping inside, but it felt like their eyes were on her. It felt like, behind their dark glasses, they were staring, their eyes cold and greedy.

The one on the left spoke, and J.D. was close enough to hear his voice, gravelly and deep. Imperious, like he was used to giving orders — and used to having them obeyed.

"We're here for the girl."

saved

J.D. forced herself to remain calm and still. She needed to look strong — she needed them to believe she wasn't afraid.

And I'm not *afraid,* she insisted silently. It was half true. *Maybe now I'll finally get some answers.*

"I'm not going back with you," she said, keeping her voice cool and level. *I am ice,* she thought, glaring at them. *I am steel.*

One of the men flinched and took a step back. The other held steady. "This isn't what you think," he said in his low, gravelly voice, and clamped a hand down on her shoulder. "We're here to help."

J.D. knocked his arm away. "Don't touch me!"

The man patted a bulge at his hip. "This is a tranquilizer gun," he said in a low monotone. "Quite fast. *Probably* harmless, though if it were me, I wouldn't want to risk it. But you're coming with us, one way or another."

Play along, she told herself. *Play along until you get your chance.*

So she stood up. The cops watched — with curiosity, not concern — as the men in black led her through the station and out the door. The one with the trank gun walked on her left, his hand pressing lightly against her lower back. The silent one kept pace on the other side, walking close, but not close enough that their arms touched. He was careful to keep a small distance between them; J.D. got the feeling he would have been happy to stand even farther away.

"We know who you are, J.D.," the man on the left said. His hair was dark and cut close and flat across the top of his head, like a military buzz. The dark glasses hid most of his face. "We know where you came from, and we're not taking you back there. We're not with LysenCorp. We're not with Sykes."

"Yeah," the other guy said, speaking for the first time. He flashed a badge, but snapped it shut before J.D. could read what it said. "We're the good guys."

"Whatever you say," J.D. muttered. They opened

the back door of a long black car. J.D. hesitated. The two men were taller than her, broader and stronger, and probably knew how to fight. They had weapons. They had the cops on their side.

We're the good guys, he had said.

They had badges.

The man with the gravelly voice pointed at the other man and jerked his eyes toward the driver's seat. The other man nodded and backed away. He got behind the wheel, slamming the door shut behind him.

And then there were two.

What's he going to do? J.D. thought, her muscles tensing. *What's he going to do that he doesn't want the other guy to see?*

"J.D." The man didn't touch her, didn't make a move to threaten her. He just stood there in front of the open car door, blocking her escape path. "J.D., look at me."

And he took off his sunglasses, revealing wide brown eyes. Eyes she knew.

"J.D.," *he whispered from the shadows.* "I'm here to help." *And then he lunged at her and grabbed her and strangled her and pressed the cloth to her mouth and she breathed in the sickly sweet chemicals and everything went gray and dizzy . . . And then she stared at his throat and wished that it would close up, squeeze shut, bleed his breath away — and it happened. He gasped. His face paled. Their eyes met, his awash in terror. A distraction, the connection broke, and he ran away. Disappeared into the shadows.*

"You." She gasped.

"I was trying to help you then, J.D., just like I'm trying to help you now. And they're on their way. If you don't get in the car and come with me, you'll be going with *them*."

Them. Ansel Sykes. LysenCorp. This guy knew who they were — and wasn't one of them.

The guy had tried to kidnap her when she was in Sykes's possession. *The enemy of my enemy is . . . my friend?*

"I don't know how much you've figured out about these people," the man said, slipping his dark glasses back on his face. "But I assure you that when *they* find you, they won't be so friendly."

She didn't know what to do. She didn't know what to believe. She didn't know how much of a risk she could afford to take. But there was only one way to find out.

She got in the car.

J.D. slammed backward against the seat as the car sped into motion. "Where are you taking me?" she demanded. "Hello?" She rapped her fist against the black partition separating her from the front seat. *"Hello?"*

"Bulletproof," a scratchy voice said. She traced it to a speaker just over her head. "And you'll find the doors are locked. For your own protection, of course."

"Can you hear me?" she yelled. There were no buttons by the speaker, no obvious microphone for her to speak into.

"Yes. You don't have to yell." The voice sounded like the one in charge, the one she had recognized from the alley. It wasn't exactly the sound of his voice, it was the tone. Confident and in control, like he knew she would eventually go along with whatever he wanted.

"Who are you?" J.D. asked quietly, not really expecting an answer.

"We're with the government," the voice said.

"What's that supposed to mean? What part of the government? And you say you want to help me — but how?"

"I can't disclose the name of our agency," the voice said. "But we've been following your case for quite a while now. We know what's been done to you. We've been working for a long time to stop it."

"Stop it how?" J.D. asked, pretending she knew what "it" was. Her heart beat even faster. Did he know about Ansel Sykes's brainwashing? About the things he'd made her do? Did he know how to stop the music, or how to keep her from losing control?

"There'll be time for all that when we get to the safe house," the voice said, infuriatingly calm. J.D. wanted to pound on the speaker, demand some answers. He was talking like he knew everything — who she was, where she'd come from, why they were after her. Everything. And all he was giving her were these bland, cryptic responses that told her nothing? After everything she'd been through, to have the answers so close, but still out of her reach . . . it was unbearable.

"How do I know you're not with LysenCorp?" she asked, even though she had already decided it was probably true. Ansel Sykes would have no reason to fool her again, not now that she knew the truth about him. She'd seen that for herself, when the woman had shot her and thrown her in the back of a van, ready to ship her off to somewhere terrible. The woman had said they were past the lies. Whatever might have happened if she hadn't escaped, J.D. guessed it wouldn't have been subtle. It would have been brutal.

"You'll just have to trust us," the voice in the speaker said.

But she didn't do that anymore; she'd learned her lesson.

The ride wore on and on, and the voice didn't speak again. The windows were tinted, turning the outside world into a stream of fuzzy blurs. She tried to follow their progress in her mind. *Right turn,* she thought, *then left,* then, after what felt like six or seven blocks, *another right.* So many turns, starts and stops, and then for a long stretch, a smooth, straight drive. They were moving faster. *A highway,* she thought. But which one? And to where?

She wrapped her fingers around the door handle and wondered what would happen if she pulled. The voice had said the door was locked, but maybe the voice had lied. Maybe if she tugged the handle, the door would swing open, and she could fling herself out onto the road. Maybe even if the door was locked, she could open it.

She pulled the handle.

The door was locked.

What would you have done? she asked herself bitterly. It was so stupid. What would have happened if the door had swung open? She pictured herself smashing onto the asphalt, another car speeding down the lane without seeing her. She pictured herself as a bloody lump of roadkill. Like a skunk. *Next time, think first,* she told herself. Even if she had survived, then what? Run away, again? She didn't even know who she was running from. Government agents? It could be another lie, but what if . . .

She didn't want to let herself think it. She would be stupid to believe them. But she couldn't help wondering. What if they really were the good guys, here to rescue her?

The car stopped.

The door opened.

"*This* is the safe house?" she asked. They were parked before a crumbling two-story house with boarded-up windows. Graffiti stained the peeling gray paint.

"Gotta find a place where no one will look for you," said the man with the gravelly voice. "You'll be safe here."

The house door opened and another man rushed out, squat and broad with thick, sturdy legs like tree trunks. Unlike the two men from the car, he was wearing a loose flannel shirt and green camouflage pants. Also unlike the two men from the car, he was carrying a gun. Not a tranquilizer gun, a real one. "This her?"

The gravelly-voiced man nodded.

"You said she'd be knocked out," the new man complained. The other one, the driver, still didn't speak.

"She's not. Deal with it." A cell phone rang, and the gravelly-voiced man snatched it out of his pocket. "What?"

J.D. could hear the small, tinny voice coming out of the phone's speaker.

"Do you have the merchandise?"

"Got it," the man said. "It'll be ready for delivery tomorrow, right on schedule." He snapped the phone shut and smiled at J.D. "Let's get you settled in." He glanced over his shoulder at the narrow road. The house was bordered on both sides by a grove of skinny trees, naked and wizened by the winter cold. But even without leaves, they were too dense for her to see what lay on the other side. Maybe more houses, maybe nothing. Still, the man looked nervous, drumming his fingers impatiently against the hood of the car. "We wouldn't want anyone seeing you out here."

J.D. touched the back of her neck, running her fingers lightly along the LysenCorp tattoo — the brand. The tiny black symbol that marked her as LysenCorp's property.

Its merchandise.

He said "it," she thought, the last slivers of hope fading away. *But he meant* me.

"Tomorrow?" the flannel-shirt guy asked. "You didn't say anything about overnight! What if she —"

"Shut up!" the gravelly-voiced man snapped.

"You're gonna give me some kind of guarantee that this isn't going to blow up in our faces, or —"

"Or what?" The man in charge glowered at him, and the silent driver flinched. But the man in the flannel shirt looked unafraid.

"Or maybe I don't play my part in this little —"

The man with the gravelly voice whipped out his heavy tranquilizer gun and slammed it into the other man's forehead. There was a whimper of surprise and pain. Then he crumpled to the ground. The gravelly-voiced man, never taking his eyes off J.D.

and never dropping his smile, knelt down and picked up the other gun. The real gun.

Government agents don't act like this, she thought. She *knew.*

She ran.

The driver grabbed J.D. roughly. He curled an arm around her waist.

"You don't want to run from me," said the man with the guns.

J.D. forced her fear down and let her anger take over. More lies, more enemies hoping she'd be stupid enough to trust them. Enough.

"*You* don't want to do that," she said, glaring back at him. She pointed at his chest. "You say you know what I am. That means you know what I can do." She flicked her hand, trying to send him flying. Nothing happened.

The man holding her finally spoke. "Boss, maybe we should . . ."

But the boss just laughed. "You can drop the act, J.D. You can't do anything to us."

She wouldn't accept that.

She focused on him and flexed her fingers — and nothing happened. *Do it,* she told herself, but it was just like trying to force herself to remember her past. You couldn't *try* to remember who you were, you couldn't *work* at it. You just did it — or you didn't.

And maybe, deep down, she didn't want it to work. *I have to hurt him,* she thought desperately. *I have to escape.* But she didn't *want* to hurt him, even after everything that had happened, and everything she feared would happen next; she didn't want to hurt anyone. Now that she knew without a doubt she had the power to do it, she was afraid. She tried to focus on the man, but all she could see were the images in her mind, the pipe falling toward Daniel's head. Mel's shoulder cracking against the pavement. Her mother, lying still.

She was more afraid of herself than she was of him — of what she might do if she lost control.

She told herself it didn't matter, that she had to let go, that she had to *fight.* But it was no use. The fear paralyzed her, kept her power locked up tight, kept her from hurting him — kept her from saving herself.

"You don't know what kind of power I have," she said, trying to keep the desperation out of her voice.

"Correction. You *used* to have power," the man said, still laughing.

"I had it in the alley," she reminded him. "I almost killed you."

"An accident," the man said, waving his hand like it was nothing. "If you could do it again, you would have already. A weapon's only as good as the control you've got over it. And we both know very well you've got none."

A new feeling flooded over her, muting the anger and the fear. It was failure. "How?" she asked quietly. "How can you know that?"

"Trust me, J.D.," the man said, but this time it didn't sound like he cared if she did or not. He smiled cruelly. "We know everything."

choice

"Let me out of here!" she screamed. Her throat was hoarse. Her fists were sore from pounding the door. There was no point in shouting — no one was coming to save her. But she didn't know what else to do.

"Just relax," they had told her, twisting her arms behind her back and marching her into the house. It was musty and damp, and the floorboards creaked like they might give out at any moment. But the rotted wood had held as they dragged her up the stairs. And when they shoved her into the tiny room, the thick wooden door slammed shut behind her, and she heard the shiny new padlock click into place. "Get some sleep!" the man had ordered through the door. "In the morning, everything will be taken care of."

He wouldn't answer any more questions, not now

that he'd proven that she was powerless and he was the one in control. He had laughed all the way up the stairs, laughed while he was shoving her into the room and locking her up. Laughed at her tears and at her screams and at the way she flailed and kicked, trying to escape. He had just squeezed tighter, lifting her off the ground when she refused to walk any farther, so that the tips of her sneakers carved out thin tracks on the dusty floor. His laugh was just as deep and gravelly as his speaking voice, like there were pebbles lodged in his throat, chewing up all his words before he spit them out.

"See you in the morning," he had said, still laughing as she pounded her fists against the door and screamed. "Until then, shut up."

The room was only a little larger than the bathroom in her fake mother's house. But while that room had been a sea of soothing blues, all shaggy carpeting and billowing curtains, this room was hard and bare. Like a jail cell. There was one small window that looked out on the grove of dead trees. The glass was jagged and broken, and the loose window frame rattled in the wind. But it was too small for her to fit through, and the iron bars prevented her from trying. The wood floor was covered with a gritty layer of dirt, and the walls were a sickly gray. There was no source of light except the tiny window, and as the sun sank beneath the horizon, the shadows came out to play.

The room was totally empty except for a small mattress shoved up against the wall. J.D. sat down on the edge; the mattress whined beneath her weight. *I can't stay here,* she thought, shivering in the draft that blew through the open window. A long, thin metal pole ran from floor to ceiling, radiating heat, but it wasn't enough to warm the room. Especially not as the sun disappeared.

She should have been able to open the door with her mind, she knew that. And she had already tried, countless times. It was useless.

Even so, she tried again, taking a deep breath and walking back across the room. As if standing in front of the door would help. But just in case it would, she put her palms flat against the cold wood and wished.

That's what it felt like, at least: wishing. Just as childish, and just as pointless. She had opened the door, she reminded herself, back in the alley. When she needed it, she had found the power inside of her and figured out how to use it. She could do it again. Somehow. She dug into herself, searching for the hidden reserve. *Going on a treasure hunt,* she thought to herself in a singsong tinged with hysteria.

It never worked when she was thinking about it, when she was struggling within herself to find the key. It exploded out of her only when her mind was clouded with anger and panic, when she forgot everything around her, when she lost herself in the moment.

And that was true in the dreams, too, she realized — the memories. She was always calm at the moment of destruction, but she wasn't thinking. She wasn't trying. She just *acted*. She let everything else go.

But how was she supposed to stop thinking now? How was she supposed to stop struggling, stop worrying, stop trying?

The harder she tried to clear her mind, the more her thoughts crowded in, battering her brain. There was no calm, no release, no abandon, only frustration. And the sense that time was running out.

"Let me out!" she screamed again. She wouldn't sit quietly, waiting for the end.

Footsteps thudded up the stairs and paused at her

door. "Shut your mouth!" the gravelly-voiced man shouted.

"Or what?" she growled back. "You'll kill me? Thought you were the good guys." Her mouth twisted on the words, and she forced herself to laugh. Let him think she wasn't afraid. Let him think he disgusted her, with his guns and his threats and his lies.

"You shut up, now," he said in a loud, level voice. "You're giving me a headache. The rest of them may be afraid of you, but I'm not. If you could get out, you would have already. But you can't, can you? You can't do anything."

"I can do more than you think!" she shouted back.

"If you don't shut up right now, I'm coming in. And you *don't* want that."

J.D. glanced over at the broken window and the iron bars, and realized, yes, she did want that.

"Let me *out*!" she shrieked, louder than before, as loud as she could. She rushed silently to the window and, wrapping her sleeve around her hand, snapped off a piece of glass. It broke off more easily than she would have expected.

J.D. crept back behind the door, raised the jagged piece of glass, and waited. She didn't want to hurt anyone — and she wouldn't hurt him much. But she would do what she needed to do to escape. There was nothing wrong with that, she told herself. But the glass felt very sharp in her hand, and very deadly. She took a deep breath.

He could have the gun, she thought suddenly at the last minute. *The real gun.* But she knew he wouldn't hurt her — at least, probably not. She was too valuable. She was "merchandise."

And she was desperate. So she would have to risk it.

"You better open this door right now!" she shrieked, even louder than before. "Just let me out! Now! Out! Please! Please! PLEEEEEEEEEEEEEEEASE!"

"I warned you —" The door flew open.

J.D. stabbed down with the shard of glass. It sliced through the air, then sank into skin — and she pulled back in horror. Cursing, the man knocked her arm out of the way, and the glass flew out of her hand, shattering on the floor. A bright stream of blood ran down his arm, soaking through his white shirt. They both stared at it in shock.

Then J.D. lunged for the door, but the man moved too fast and shoved her out of the way. She staggered back, her head slamming into the wall. A sharp pain shot through her and tears sprang to her eyes as everything went blurry.

"You little brat!" the man growled, whipping out a pair of handcuffs. He slammed one cuff around her wrist, then dragged her into the corner and wrapped her arms around the heating pipe. She squealed as her skin brushed the blisteringly hot metal, but he ignored her, locking her other wrist into the cuff. "You like this better?" he shouted, bending down so that his eyes met hers and his breath blew hot on her face.

J.D. opened her mouth to shout back at him — and he stuffed something into it, something thick and furry and foul. She gagged and tried to spit it out, but his hand squeezed down on her head. He pushed her forward, so that her cheek was nearly pressed against the metal pipe. She winced at the heat. "Another inch, and you burn," he warned. "Get it?"

She couldn't speak with the gag in her mouth and couldn't nod with his hand holding her still. So she just moaned and went limp. He smiled and nodded. "Good girl." He pulled a roll of duct tape from one of the pockets on his carpenter jeans. He'd changed out of the fancy suit, she noticed. Because he no longer had to pretend.

He tore off a piece of tape and slapped it across her mouth, sealing the foul cloth inside. She nearly gagged as it tickled the back of her throat.

Don't throw up, she warned herself desperately. *You'll choke.*

You'll die.

The man patted her on the back. "I'm feeling better already. My headache's almost gone. How 'bout you?"

She couldn't speak; she didn't dare move.

He nodded. "Like I said, better already. Enjoy your night."

The door slammed shut, the lock clicked into place, and she was alone.

J.D.'s muscles unclenched, and she let her arms droop in relief. But they grazed against the hot pipe, and it burned. She jerked her wrists away, holding her arms straight out ahead of her. There was only so long she'd be able to hold them up. Only so long she'd be able to stand. She closed her eyes against the waves of heat radiating off the pipe. *I have to get out of here,* she thought, trying to keep the panic away.

Holding the cuff steady with her left hand, she tried to slip her right wrist out of its metal cage. Her wrists were so thin, and there was almost enough space, if she could just pull hard enough, if she could bear the sharp metal scraping against her skin . . .

A bead of blood bloomed on her wrist, then another, and she stopped tugging. The raw pain didn't go away.

This is it, she thought, wanting to curl up in a ball and go to sleep, even if it would mean resting her body against the scalding pole. *I give up.*

But she didn't. She couldn't. This wasn't a game, this wasn't a test, this was life — and somehow she knew that this was her last chance. That when morning came, and the "merchandise" was handed over to whoever was buying her, that would be it.

Focus, she told herself. *Concentrate.*

This was *her* brain, *her* body. She wasn't anyone's property. She was in power. She was in control. She just needed to find that place in her mind, to unlock it, force it to do what she needed it to do.

Focus.

She pushed away her terror, stopped thinking about the men behind the door and their guns and whatever lay ahead of her when morning came. She stopped worrying about what would happen — what she might do — if she lost control. No more fear. No more anger. No more.

Focus.

She stopped wondering what would happen next if she couldn't unlock the cuffs. Stopped trying to remember all the things she'd forgotten. Stopped thinking about Daniel and the long lecture he'd given her about locks, about climbing inside of them, learning their works, splitting them open. Stopped thinking at all.

Focus.

There was no more time for thought, no room for it. Instead, she felt. She felt the hard edges of the cuffs digging into her wrists, hot from the pipe, sharp, solid. She felt her heart thudding in her chest and the tightness in her lungs as she struggled for breath. Felt the gag lodged in her mouth, rough and furry, her tongue forced against her bottom jaw, the duct tape holding her skin taut, forcing her lips into a flat smile.

Focus.

Felt the tired muscles in her arms, straining away from the heat, felt her hands, warm from the pipe, and warmer still from something inside, something building, power. She felt it deep inside of her, waiting. Waiting for her to set it free. She felt it and she knew it, like it had always been there, and she let it go.

A rush of heat, a rush of fire, of power, and the cuffs snapped open, and she was free.

Without pausing to think, she ripped off the tape and spit out the sock and crossed the room. The door flew open, like it was nothing. She could feel the power inside of her, she felt like she was glowing, like she could do anything — and then she heard the voices, and she stopped.

Run, she thought. That was the smart thing to do. Run.

Or fight.

Her body wanted action. The power within her wanted to play, wanted to stretch its legs, see what it could do. Wanted to take control.

Her skin tingled and crackled like it was on fire. But she forced herself to stand still. She took one deep breath, then another. And slowly, almost painfully, the fog disappeared, and she came back to herself. Thought crept back into her head. The power faded away, but she could feel it lurking beneath the surface, and she could feel how thin that surface was, how fragile. And she knew she could get it back when she needed it. She was in charge.

So what next?

Run, she thought again. *Just get out. Go. Hide.* But

go where? Hide from what? For how long? She had spent too much time running, too much time hiding out, waiting for answers that would never come. The answers were here, right here, waiting for her, if she was brave enough to face them.

She couldn't keep running from shadows. She needed to find out who the enemy really was, so that, when the time came, she would be ready to face it.

So she would be ready to fight.

J.D. huddled on the stairwell, her elbows propped on her knees, held herself very still, and listened.

She holds her breath. If they catch her, she will be in so much trouble, but she must know. The house twinkles like starlight and smells like Christmas, sweet and cozy, like her home is made of gingerbread. But Christmas is still so far away, and she can't wait, she must know what is in the beautiful gold and silver boxes.

A bicycle?

A new pair of roller skates?

The RoboPuppy with a special chip that lets it walk and wag its tail and bark, that she wants more than anything in the world except . . .

A real puppy? Had Mommy and Daddy finally given in?

She strains to hear. Their voices float up from the kitchen, happy and soft, too soft to hear. And then it wells up inside of her, and she presses her finger under her nose and holds her breath until she thinks her lungs are going to burst, but the sneeze explodes out of her.

Aaaaah —

J.D. held her breath and swallowed the sneeze, trying to shake herself back to reality. The memories were still so vivid, so real, even now that she knew they were nothing more than pretty lies. She still felt like that child on the stairs. She still missed her mother.

But that was a lie; *this* was real.

She could hear all three of them down in the kitchen. The gravelly-voiced man. The high-voiced driver. And the third man must have been the one in flannel, the one who she'd last seen lying unconscious on the front lawn.

"This is a mistake," the man in flannel said. "This is gonna go bad, I can feel it."

"Why don't you go get some sleep," the gravelly voice suggested. "It'll all be over in the morning."

"You think I can *sleep*?" the first one said, his voice rising even higher. "With that, that *thing* upstairs?"

J.D. forced herself not to move, not to make a sound.

"Thing." It shouldn't have mattered. But it hurt.

"I told you, she's harmless," the boss said.

"Harmless?" The driver, his voice high and tense, started to laugh. "Boss, she's a weapon. They designed her to be the perfect weapon — undetectable. Unstoppable. Harmless? I don't think so."

"That's right, the perfect weapon," the gravelly-voiced man said. "Which makes her invaluable. We just make it through to morning, hand her over to the buyer, and we'll be set for life."

J.D. didn't want to believe what she was hearing, but it felt right. It confirmed her deepest fears, the ones she hadn't wanted to admit to herself. She wasn't normal. Maybe she wasn't even *human*. Ansel Sykes had designed her as a weapon and — she remembered the horrifying things she'd seen in her dreams — he had used her to kill.

What if she'd *liked* the destruction, craved the killing?

What if that's who she had been before she lost her memory — and who she might become, if Sykes got her back?

"Still feels kind of weird," said the driver. "Selling a kid."

"She's not a kid." The gravel in his voice turned to rock. "She's . . . something else. They all are. I saw that much, before they threw me out of the LysenCorp Institute. I'm telling you, they're all freaks. Designed to look normal maybe, but deep down . . . freaks. And this one's the worst of all."

"They?" J.D. thought. There were *others* like her?

J.D. crept down the stairs as quietly as she could. She'd heard enough; it was time to go. But she would have to pass through the kitchen to get to the front door. She would have to get by the men.

I can do it, she thought, feeling the power simmering. She'd been designed to be a weapon, so why not fulfill her destiny?

She pictured the men flying across the room, slamming into the wall. She pictured the gravelly-voiced man crashing onto the floor. Staring up at her with fear in his eyes. Fear and respect.

Yes, she could do it.

She could almost see the blood, could almost hear the screams — and it made her sick.

I don't want to be a weapon. I don't want to hurt anyone.

Not even them.

She could access her power now, she was sure of that. She could control it. And she didn't want anyone else to die.

There was a hallway at the bottom of the stairwell, and she crept along it, away from the kitchen. It opened into a small, dark room. Shadowy mounds of furniture covered by dusty sheets dotted the room, lit up by a glint of moonlight.

The light streamed through a window — a window with no bars and no boards. She tugged, but it wouldn't open. The wood had warped, and the frame was stuck.

J.D. paused. She needed to break the glass. There were shapes beneath the sheets that looked like chairs. She could find something she could use. But something told her she didn't need it.

She raised her hand. Focused. Held her breath.

The glass shattered.

Pain streaked her thigh as she scraped against a shard of glass jutting from the frame. She ignored it, and ignored the hot trickle of blood down her leg. Climbed through, and let herself down to the lawn. The air was cold and crisp, the moon bright. And she was free.

Run, her body said again, and this time she obeyed.

"Stop!" one of the men called from behind her. She didn't hesitate.

"Stop or I'll shoot!"

It might have been a bluff. She was already far away, though not far enough. She was on the move. If he shot, he might miss.

But he might not. And if she ran, they would chase. Maybe she'd run enough.

She stopped.

She turned.

"Good choice," said the man with the gun. It was a real gun, dark and sleek, and pointed at her face.

"You won't shoot me," she said, her voice cool. "I'm 'invaluable,' remember?"

The gravelly-voiced man lowered the gun slightly, so it was aimed at her stomach instead of her head. "Who said I'm shooting to kill?" He smiled cruelly. "Of course, I've never had the best aim. . . ."

The other two men appeared behind him, and one took a step toward her. "Stay back," she warned. "Before I hurt you."

The man in charge didn't laugh this time, just shook his head. "This again? It's getting pathetic."

"I could tear you apart with a thought," she said. Her heart was pounding, but she felt no fear. Only anger, certainty . . . and excitement. "I could twist that gun around in your hands and send a bullet into your head. I could break your bones. Tear your muscles. I can destroy you."

The boss didn't move, but the other two looked nervous. "You're bluffing," the driver squeaked.

She stared back at them, and though she *had* been bluffing, she suddenly realized she wasn't. "Try me." The cold poison in her voice was shooting through her veins, and it felt good. It felt strong. There was fear in their eyes, and she fed on it, hungered for it, and there was a voice in her head that said, *Do it, destroy them all,* and it wasn't her voice, it was a low, deep, calm voice. It was Ansel Sykes's voice, and she wanted, more than anything, to obey.

She ran.

Not from them — from herself, from what she might do. Into the night, into the crop of trees alongside the house. Away. There was a booming crack, so loud the air seemed to shake, then another. *They're shooting at me,* she thought, *they're really trying to* kill *me.* Her last grip on the rational fell away, and the anger took over.

She whirled around, flicked a wrist, and something shifted in her mind. The gravelly-voiced man flew into the air and slammed hard into a tree. He screamed as he flew, but then there was a thud and a crash. He lay still, his eyes fluttering, moaning softly with each breath. The other two men froze, gaping first at him, then at her. "You *are* a monster," the man in the flannel shirt shouted, trembling all over. "We should have killed you when we had the chance. We'd be doing the world a favor."

How dare he?

She raised her arm, extended her fingers. His eyes widened — and he turned on his heel and ran. The other man followed a second later. J.D. lunged in their direction . . . and then stopped herself cold.

What am I doing?

But that wasn't the question, not really.

Who am I? What have I become?

Even that was a question that no longer needed to be asked. She finally had her answer. She knew what she was: a deadly weapon. And now she had proof.

return

She walked.

There was no other way. There were two other houses on the dark, narrow street. But she couldn't just walk up a stone pathway, ring a doorbell, and ask for help. What would she say? "I'm a dangerous superweapon escaped from a secret laboratory. Can you help me get away from the people who want to sell me to the highest bidder?" They would ship her off to a mental institution. Or call the cops. And she'd been there, done that. So she walked.

Down the street, away from the grime-encrusted house that looked fit only for a family of ghosts. Away from the two men huddling inside, and the third man, the man with the gravelly voice, who maybe still lay on the ground under a dying tree. She didn't want to be that person, the one who caused pain.

But did she have a choice?

They designed me, she thought. *They programmed me. So maybe I can't help who I am.*

She didn't want to believe that. She had turned away, she reminded herself. She had only hurt the man because he was shooting at her. The other two . . . she could have chased them, could have hurt them or killed them. But instead she had turned away. That had to mean something.

She walked.

What is the self, other than an accumulation of memories? Ansel Sykes had asked her once, when he was pretending to be Dr. Styron, pretending to be her friend. *We are who we are because of what has happened to us.* He had told her so many lies, but that one rang true. Whatever she'd done, whoever she was behind that blank white wall, it was no longer a part of her. She had started fresh.

I am whoever I want to be now, she told herself. *It doesn't matter who I was.* Except that it did matter.

Because Ansel Sykes was still after her, and now she knew he wasn't the only one. Everyone was after her, for what they thought she could do, for what she'd done.

Because she had found her power, but she still had the dreams, still had the visions, still heard the music — and she had done things. Terrible things, without meaning to.

Because they still owned a piece of her.

Because she didn't know who "they" were, not really. Sykes, LysenCorp, the gravelly-voiced man and his "buyer" — too many enemies, and she couldn't run forever. But she couldn't fight until she knew where to find them, and how to win.

She walked.

The car had turned left onto the street, so when the road met another, she turned right. And walked on, until she hit the highway, stretching into the darkness, silent and empty. She hugged the shoulder, her eyes tearing in the wind. A car screamed past, too close. But there was nowhere to go, only the highway and, on the other side, an embankment. A steep slope of grass and at the bottom, a creek, with icy water and jagged rocks. So she stayed on her narrow path and braced herself against the headlights, waiting for the trucks to rumble by, for the windstorm to blow past her in their wake. It began to rain.

She walked.

Her toes went numb first, as the rainwater sloshed in her sneakers, soaking her socks. There was pain,

sharp at first, and then the cold gave way to a creeping, pins-and-needles warmth. And then nothing.
She walked with her hands jammed in her pockets,
her fingers curled into fists, but the wind found
them, and they went cold and stiff, too clumsy to
button her top button or brush the sleet out of her
eyes. So she pulled her arms inside her jacket, inside
her shirt, and folded them across her body, tucking
her fingers under her armpits, where it was warm.

She walked.

Fluorescent lights lit the big green signs along the
road. Confusing signs. Exit here for Route 178. Two
miles to 276. Stay left for Hwy 14. She followed the
road and hoped. And then she saw a sign that seemed
to make sense, and she followed it. And an hour
later, she saw another.

The moon set, leaving her in total darkness. She
wasn't afraid.

The night passed, and she walked, though she
could no longer feel her feet or her ears or the tip of
her nose. It seemed like the sky should have turned
orange, that the stars should have faded into a pink-
and-yellow haze. But the sun was still hiding. The
night had turned from navy to black to gray, but

the world was still in shadow. And when the city lights appeared, sparkling, scraping the sky, it was still dark enough for them to shine.

The peaks of the city loomed, sharply angled towers that jutted up and down like a mouthful of broken teeth. She had made it.

The city would never be safe, but she could slip across its borders and lose herself in the crowds. She could start her search, a real search this time, for answers that she was ready to fight for and pursuers she was ready to face. Ready to defeat. The city was a place to start. A familiar place, to rest, to hide, to regroup. It was a place she knew, as much as she knew anywhere. It was the only place she had a past.

But that didn't make it home.

Daniel won't be there, she told herself. Then she told herself that it wouldn't matter if he was. The shell of the old factory was gray and hulking in the predawn light, a cinder-block fortress. It even had a moat, of sorts, if you counted the no-man's-land of gravel and cracked cement winding around its edges, dotted with billowing trash and burned-out cars.

If you counted the guy slumped against the Dumpster, his eyes a bloody red and his breath like fire, it even had a dragon.

But J.D. was undeterred. She had a mission, was on a quest for the holy grail of warmth and sleep. And if anyone recognized her, if anyone was tempted to turn her in . . . so what? She'd tested herself in battle; she'd proven herself worthy.

She knocked.

There was a secret knock, a pattern that shifted every few days.

Tap. Tap-tap-tap. Tap. Tap-tap.

There was no answer. The code must have shifted. But J.D. was too tired to try again. She raised an arm, flicked a wrist, felt deep in her mind.

The door opened.

"What the — ?" A figure stepped into her way. *"You."*

J.D. had never trusted Jacob, but after everything she'd been through, she was almost ready to try. Just for a few moments, just for a calm, quiet night. He'd been so kind, so encouraging, so gentle —

His lips twisted into a snarl, and he grabbed the door, would have slammed it shut in her face if she hadn't stuck her foot in the way. "You can't be here. Get out."

"What?" It was so unexpected — his face, his tone, his *anger* — that J.D. didn't know how to react. "Why?"

"I know you went to the cops. What did you tell them?"

"*Went* to the cops? Daniel *sicced* them on me!"

"Daniel left here to find you, and you were both spotted with the cops, but somehow he's gone and *you've* mysteriously found your way back here? Nice try. Get out."

"Jacob, what's your problem?"

"What did you tell them about me?" he asked, his voice a low, dangerous growl. This wasn't the same Jacob she remembered, the one who'd saved her when Tec held a knife to her throat. This, she realized, was the Jacob who had armed Tec with that knife in the first place. "About us?"

"Look, what would I tell them? I don't even know anything about you," J.D. protested. "And besides, what do they care about a bunch of runaways hanging out in an old factory?"

Jacob spit out a laugh. "Oh, grow up, J.D. You know we're not just 'hanging out.' How do you think we pay for that food you stuffed down and that sleeping bag that kept you warm? You think it just came from the blanket fairy?"

J.D.'s teeth were chattering so hard it was difficult to talk. She forced her muscles to still. "Look, I don't know what you're doing here, and I don't care. I didn't tell the cops anything. I just need a place to crash for the night, and this is it."

"Think again," he said, and then gentle, generous, you-can-trust-me Jacob drew back his jacket to reveal the switchblade poking out of his pocket. He rested his right hand lightly on its handle, his thumb playing over the button that would extend the blade. "If the cops sent you back here to get more information, you can just crawl back to them and tell them it's not going to happen."

She could have walked away, probably should have walked away, but she had walked too far and too long. Now was the time for rest. "I'm not going anywhere, Jacob." She flexed her fingers, fixed her gaze on the knife. "One way or another, I'm coming in."

"You don't want to push me, J.D."

She had thought she was exhausted; she had thought she was ready to drop. But it turned out she was still in a pushing mood. "I promise you,

Jacob, you *want* to let me in," she warned in a low voice. She shook her head. "I don't want to threaten you. You wouldn't believe me anyway. But you don't have to believe me. I am coming in, and I'm staying."

"Dude, is that J.D.?" An eager, high voice piped up from the shadows. Tec appeared at the door, elbowing Jacob out of the way. "You're back! What are you doing outside? It's freezing. Come in."

"She's not —"

"I was just about to," J.D. said loudly, and stepped past Jacob. Let him try to stop her in front of his adoring flock. Let him see how far his authority would stretch if he tried to attack a defenseless girl in a paranoid rage. Let him see what happened when the girl fought back.

"You look exhausted," Jacob said, and when she looked back at him, his face had transformed. The eyes were soft and wide, the forehead smooth, the mouth pulled back in an easy smile. "Tec, why don't you set up a spot for her to sleep, and I'll rustle up something for her to eat."

"And then you'll tell us where you went and what happened to Daniel, right?" Tec said.

"Tec, go." Jacob's warning was gentle, without

even an undercurrent of danger. Tec followed orders immediately. "Only one day," he told J.D., and his voice was steel again. "You can sleep as much as you need to, but as soon as you're up, you're gone. Got it?"

She didn't answer him.

She just brushed past him and followed Tec across the wide room to a warm and cozy corner. He gestured to an empty sleeping bag. She pulled off her soaking-wet jacket, slipped out of her sneakers, and wrapped herself in the soft flannel bag with a sigh.

The girl lying next to it opened her eyes and sat up.

"What'd you do to him?" the girl asked as soon as she'd rubbed away the sleep.

J.D. recognized the hostility in the voice almost before she recognized the face. Andi. "Who?"

She rolled her eyes. "Daniel. He went off looking for you, and he never came back."

"I, uh, think they sent him back. To the Center."

Andi looked like she wanted to spit. "That's your fault, you know. I told him he should stay here, but he just *had* to go find you. Whatever happens to him now, that's on you."

"Somehow, I think I can live with myself," J.D. said, and tried to mean it. She didn't care what happened to Daniel now, not after he'd betrayed her.

He didn't mean to, something inside her said, but that part of her was soft and too kind, and she pushed it down. She held its head under until it ran out of breath and gave up the fight. She was tougher than she'd been before. Stronger. She didn't need him anymore. And she definitely didn't need *Andi's* forgiveness.

J.D. turned her back on the other girl and gave Tec a thin smile. "Thanks. I've got to get some sleep, so . . ."

Tec wasn't looking at her. He was looking at Andi. "Don't you think you should —"

"Just keep your mouth shut about stuff that's none of your business," Andi snapped.

"Like it's *yours*?" Tec asked.

"What do you care?"

J.D. wanted to ask what they were talking about — knowing, somehow, that they were talking about her. But it didn't seem important. Nothing seemed important as she toppled down on the sleeping bag, the warm flannel drawing her in. It was like a bed of feathers, of plush velvet by a roaring fire, and it was so soft, so warm, and she was so tired . . .

She opened her mouth to ask the question, the words struggling through a fog of exhaustion, climbing onto her tongue, but it was so much work. Too much work. And she was finally warm; she was finally still.

She let sleep win the fight.

She swung a fist at her attacker.

"Hey, chill, it's just me!"

She opened her eyes. The room was bright with a yellowy afternoon light. Tec knelt over her, arms shielding his face in case of another stray punch.

"Sorry," she mumbled. The old factory was mostly empty — she must have slept most of the day away. But somehow she still felt too tired to move. She wiggled her toes. They still worked, at least, and she could feel them again. But all she could feel was pain. Sharp and stabbing pains in her toes, and in her calves when she tried to move her legs, a dull ache in her back when she tried to sit up.

"Jacob left me here to watch you," Tec said. "He told me to wake you up at three, said you had somewhere to go, but . . . What's going on, J.D.? Where are you going?"

"It's complicated." She rubbed her eyes, then her upper arm, where a row of purpling bruises had bloomed on the pale skin. *Fingerprints,* she thought. *They marked me.* "But I should probably . . ."

"Wait." He reached up to grab her, but she jerked away, and without thinking, raised her arms, ready to send him flying, to hurt him before he could hurt her.

It's just Tec, she reminded herself, just in time.

She lowered her arms. When had she become so eager to pull the trigger?

"I got something for you," he said, pulling something out of his pocket and holding his hands behind his back.

"Like — a present?"

He wrinkled his nose. "Like — no." He thrust out his fist, then opened it, revealing a scrunched envelope on his palm. "Someone gave it to Andi, told her to give it to you if you showed up here again. But" — he shrugged — "you know Andi."

"Not really."

Tec's face lit up with a mischievous grin. It made him look like a little kid, and J.D. suddenly wondered how old he really was and how he'd ended up on his own. "I knew where she was hiding it, and I just figured . . . it's yours, right? You should see it."

He handed her the crumpled envelope. "Sorry it's kind of . . ."

"Thanks, Tec."

They stared at each other. He was bouncing gently on his toes, like a kid on Christmas morning. "Aren't you going to open it?"

"Well . . ." J.D. scratched her ear and tapped her finger against the envelope, waiting for him to get the hint. But his eyes were bright and wide, and totally clueless. "I should probably look at it alone. If that's okay."

"Oh. Yeah, sure." He backed away, plopped down on his own sleeping bag, and pulled out a torn comic book. "I'll just. You know. Be over here." His face glowed pink.

"Hey, Tec?"

"Yeah?" he mumbled.

"Seriously. Thanks for giving me this. You're a really good guy."

"Well, I figured I owed you one. You know, after . . . how we met."

J.D. smiled. Then she looked at the envelope, and the smile disappeared.

It said nothing but "J.D.," in thick block letters.

It's from Daniel, she thought. Knew. It was some kind of explanation, or an apology, or maybe a rant about how she had no right to be angry with him. An attempt to protest, once again, that he was just trying to help.

Because he was.

She was afraid of what it might say, afraid of opening the letter and finding out that she still cared. That he did, too.

She was afraid of finding out that he didn't.

She smoothed out the envelope, stuck her finger in the seam, and, very slowly, very neatly, ripped it open. Pulled out a folded sheet of white paper. Sucked in a deep breath, and unfolded the letter.

Disappointment struck first.

Then confusion.

Then hope.

It wasn't from Daniel.

When you've got nowhere left to run:
609-555-7878

The rest of the sheet was blank, except for one small mark in the upper right-hand corner. The ink was black. So black that the symbol didn't look printed on the paper — it looked like an *absence* of paper, like in the dark of those sharp, black lines, the paper had ceased to exist:

fight

LysenCorp had found her. Sykes had found her.

He could be watching her, even now. He could be waiting just outside the door, straitjacket in one hand, tranquilizer gun in the other.

But somehow, she didn't think so.

When you've got nowhere left to run.

It was like he knew. Like he had *let* her escape, knowing she would only last so long, would come crawling back.

But he couldn't know everything. He couldn't know that she had rediscovered herself, found the power inside of her. He couldn't know that when she faced him again, it would be on *her* terms. She would be ready to fight.

The pain in her legs faded away as adrenaline flooded through her. She had been determined to seek out LysenCorp, to find Sykes and *make* him tell her who she was and what he had done to her. He had just saved her the trouble of the search.

Don't be stupid, a calmer, more rational voice in her head warned. *You just escaped — and now you want to be a prisoner again?*

She wouldn't be a prisoner. Not now that she'd learned their secret. She wasn't a pawn in their monstrous game. She was the queen.

The men she'd just escaped from had nothing to do with LysenCorp. She was sure of that. Sykes's operation had been well funded — enough to create a whole fake history, a house filled with photo albums and imaginary memories. The men in black with the fake badges obviously didn't have those kinds of resources. They knew about Sykes, but they weren't *with* him. Where Sykes had been smooth and subtle, they'd been crude, violent. Obvious. Sykes had wanted to deceive her, to lull her into a state of calm so he could take control. The others had just wanted to auction her off to the highest bidder — and, failing that, to hurt her. Maybe to kill her.

"J.D.? What is it, what's wrong?" Tec looked concerned, but also scared, like if he came any closer, he'd get in trouble once again.

She shook her head. "Nothing." She folded the letter and was about to put it back in the envelope — then stopped. She unfolded it again and stared at the number, running it through her mind, over and over again.

609-555-7878.

She stared at the numbers until they blurred and danced across the page, squiggling through her field of vision and through her brain. And finally, when she was sure she had it right, she tucked the letter into the envelope. Then she handed the envelope to Tec.

"If Daniel comes back —".

"If? You don't know where he is?"

"If Daniel comes back, can you . . ." Maybe she should leave him a note, but she didn't know what it would say.

I hate you?

I miss you?

I forgive you?

I'm sorry?

"Can you just give this to him?" she asked.

"But —" Something about the look on her face shut him up, and he just nodded. "Sure." He glanced at the door. "Guess you're going, too?"

She nodded.

"Ever coming back?"

"I don't know." She took a last look around at the cold, cavernous space with its rusty machinery and pigeons flapping at the corners of the high ceiling. It was dirty, and the stench of the nearby landfill made everything seem sticky and rotten. But despite that, despite Jacob and his paranoia and his switchblade, despite Andi and her bitter glares, despite the cement floors and the rickety iron pipes and gears that could puncture a foot or crash down on someone's head, there was something comforting about the place. Something that came from the stacks of comic books and empty pizza boxes, or maybe the old radio piping hip-hop and static into the air, something that felt safe.

And despite what she had said, she knew: She wouldn't be coming back.

The first pay phone she found had no dial tone. The second had no receiver, only a metal chain hanging down from the box, wires spraying out of the end. The third was encased in an old-fashioned glass phone booth, graffiti across the side announcing that HIFI SUX. The other side was just an empty frame bordered by a few remaining shards of glass.

The two guys standing on the corner looked ready to break the other pane of glass — with her inside.

I'm not afraid, J.D. repeated to herself. It was her new slogan; it kept her going, putting one foot in front of the other. *Not anymore.*

She stepped into the booth, turning her back to the guys on the corner, and pulled a quarter out of her pocket. Tec had given it to her like it was nothing, but she knew it was probably all he had that day. She promised herself she would pay him back.

The debts were mounting up.

It smelled like moldy cabbage inside the booth, and the phone had a wad of gum stuck to the handle. She held her breath and pulled her sleeve over her hand, so she wouldn't have to touch the germ-ridden plastic. She slipped the quarter into the slot.

Do I really want to do this?

She punched the buttons.

Six.

Zero. Nine. Five.

She paused. Not because she couldn't remember — as always, her memory was perfect, except when it was nonexistent.

Five. Five.

Seven eight seven.

She stopped again.

Maybe I don't need more answers, she thought. *Maybe I know enough.*

She knew there were people out there who wanted to hurt her. She knew they had "designed" her to be a weapon, and they had done their job well. She knew that, in her old life, she had been a freak. Maybe a monster. She had hurt people. And — she remembered the flashbacks she'd had, injections of a green liquid that burned from the inside out — she had been hurt as well.

She had lost her past. Maybe, like Daniel said, that was a blessing. Maybe she didn't need to know who she really was. She could start fresh. Go back to the hideout, talk Jacob into letting her stay. Or find Daniel again, make things right. She could go back to the Center, she could go anywhere. She was no longer trapped by her fear, and that meant she was free. This was her moment of choice, and maybe she should choose to start again.

But J.D.'s memories of the past few days were too strong and too bright, and she couldn't forget what she had heard, hiding in that tiny stairwell, trying not to make a sound.

"She's something else," they had said about her.

Not just a girl, not a harmless kid. Maybe not even completely human. Definitely not normal. Something else. "They all are."

They.

The others like her.

Others who would understand. Others who shared her powers, her problems, others who could share her life.

Not like Daniel. Even if she could trust him again, she couldn't drag him down, couldn't put him in danger when he had the chance to be happy and safe without her. Daniel had the chance to be normal. J.D. never would. But if, somewhere, there were others just like her, maybe it didn't matter.

What if she didn't have to be alone?

Eight.

There was a moment of silence after she pressed the final number, and then the line began to ring. The blast of sound was like a siren in her ear. Once. Twice. It rang and rang until she stopped counting, but she refused to hang up. This was her last, best link to the truth. And then the ringing stopped. Someone picked up the phone.

She could hear him breathe.

But he said nothing.

"Hello?" Her voice was shaking.

There was no answer.

The seconds passed, and all she could hear was his breathing, low and even.

"Hello?" she said again. "Say something!"

The heavy stench in the booth was making her nauseous. And the silence stretched on. Was this it? Another dead end? Some kind of joke?

"Say something!" she shouted, her grip tightening around the receiver. "Is this Sykes? Is it you? Hello? You're the one who told me to call. What do you want from me? *What do you want from me?!*"

The line went dead.

She was disgusted with herself for losing control. She wouldn't let Sykes do this to her. She would stay calm. She would plan her next step. There were still choices, still possibilities. She just had to think.

J.D. stepped out of the booth. The guys at the corner were gone, with only a small pile of cigarette butts left behind to show they'd existed. The sidewalk was completely empty.

An unmarked white van idled at the corner. Waiting.

Its side door was open and a man stood next to it, staring down the street. Staring at J.D. She glanced at the phone booth, then back at the van. So this was it. They must have tracked her call. Or maybe they'd been following her the whole time, waiting to see if she would take the bait.

There was still time to run. The street wasn't a dead end. It stretched to an intersection, curved toward a busy shopping district, where there would be lights and noise and people. She would have a head start if she ran now. She would get away.

J.D. shoved her hands in her pockets and started down the sidewalk, kicking a large piece of broken glass along like a soccer ball.

The man was a stranger. His head was bald and shiny, his nose crooked, like he'd taken one too many punches. He wore black pants and a thin black shirt, too thin for the weather, but he didn't look cold. He didn't look like he was in the business of feeling cold, or feeling anything, for that matter. His mouth was a firm, straight line; his eyes were fixed on J.D. She couldn't pin down their color — first they seemed brown, then, as she took a step, they shifted to greenish blue. As she drew closer, she became certain they were gray.

J.D.'s fingertips tingled, and she dug her nails into

her palms. She could feel it inside of her, the power to stop him from whatever he'd been ordered to do. He worked for Sykes, she knew that, and she hated him for it. And the hate was stronger than anything else — but not stronger than her. She pushed it down. The man was just the beginning. She needed to be patient enough to reach the end.

"I'm J.D.," she said, when she got close enough. She stopped when there was still three feet of space between them. She didn't see a weapon, but she was sure he had one.

He nodded. "I know." He jerked his head toward the open door of the van, toward the darkness.

J.D. found she didn't have to pretend not to be afraid. She just wasn't. This was playing out exactly as she'd planned. The man probably thought he'd caught her. But she was the one who'd caught him. "Are you going to take me to him?" she asked. "To Sykes?"

His eyes widened, just slightly, just enough to reveal his surprise. And then his face returned to its default blankness. "You've been doing your homework," he said, raising his arm and pointing toward the open door. "Final exam time."

Last chance.

She took the final few steps toward the van. "To Sykes?" she said again.

He nodded and reached out to help her climb inside, but she shook him off. "I got it."

He shrugged and raised the handle, preparing to shut the door, to leave her stranded in the darkness. *I am not afraid,* she thought furiously, her lips moving with each word. *I am* not *afraid.*

"This is just a precaution," he said as the door slid shut and the darkness disappeared. "It sounds like you know enough to understand."

"What are you — ?"

And then an arm reached out of the darkness and grabbed her throat.

The needle slid into her skin where her neck met her shoulder blades, where the small black tattoo branded her forever. *Bull's-eye,* she had time to think as the hold on her throat relaxed and she sank down to the floor of the van.

Soft, she thought, her cheek pressed against fuzzy carpet.

Tired.

Afraid.

The van was darkness. Shadow. But her eyes slid

closed, and behind the lids, an explosion of light, a white nothingness. Like the white fog that clouded her memories, blank and smooth and endless. She struggled to grab hold of something, anything. But there was nothing to grab hold of, and she slipped away.

welcome

Pain.

Pain everywhere.

And then it narrowed to a point. Her stomach. Something hard, something rough, jabbing, jabbing. She opened her eyes, groaned at the light. *Too bright,* she thought.

Her head was fuzzy, her thoughts thick and slow. She lay on her side, and beneath her: dirt. A black boot thumped into her stomach. Several moments later, she flinched. *Too slow.*

"Time to get up."

The voice was level and impersonal, like a computer on the other end of a phone line.

Black boots. One nudged her again. Hard.

Black pants. J.D. dug her fingers into the dirt, lifted her head. Swallowed down bile as the world tilted. A black shirt. Shiny head. She knew him.

The man, she thought, breathing in hungrily. The cold air cut through the fog, peeling away the layers of confusion.

A van.

And then she remembered the needle, and she sat up. She ignored the nausea and the fog and she jumped to her feet. The panic was like a thousand knives stabbing her skin, poking and scratching and slicing, and silently, secretly, she screamed.

I can't do this, she thought, her breaths coming faster, then faster still, her heartbeat sprinting. *I thought I could, but I can't, I have to get out of here —*

"We're going inside now," the man said.

Here. The van idled in a small empty parking lot, and beyond it? A vast meadow. The grassy expanse of her nightmares. Somewhere out there, she knew, were the charred remains of a helicopter. Lights twinkled on the horizon.

"Floodlights. Electrified barbed wire. Fully automated sentry system with level-three countermeasures," the man said, following her gaze. "We call that level K, for kill. Just in case you should get any ideas."

On the other side of the lot sat an enormous white complex of low, wide buildings connected by narrow tunnels. It should have looked perfectly normal, just an industrial campus spread out along beautiful grounds. But there was something off about it.

No signs, she thought first. No symbols, no logos, no corporate insignia. She was sure this was Lysen-Corp, but there was no proof. The buildings were blank, anonymous.

And then she noticed something else: no windows.

The building in front of them must have been a hundred yards wide, but there was only one entrance. Two guards stood at the narrow doorway, one on each side. They were in uniforms, though again, there was no insignia, no identifying marks, and they were armed.

"We're going inside," the man said again, stepping toward her. "We going to do this the easy way, or the hard way?"

"Back off!" she shouted.

He flinched.

And a little of her confidence crept back in.

"I've got orders to take you inside," the man growled. "And you don't disobey orders. Not around here. You'll remember soon enough."

"I guess I'm slow," she shot back. "Because I don't see any reason to obey anything."

The man drew something out of his pocket. It wasn't a gun. It wasn't a needle. It was just a tiny, box-shaped object, the size of a remote control, with just as many buttons. "I don't want to hurt you," he said, but she could read the lie in his stormy eyes, and the way his fingers were twitching over the thing's buttons.

"I think we both know you *can't* hurt me." And she let the warmth flow through her, let her mind break clear of thought and worry, let the power build.

Not because she wanted to hurt him, but because it was easier this way. When the power was hurtling through her, there was no fear. She knew who was in control.

"You don't know as much as you think you do, kid." His finger hovered over one of the buttons. "But this should give you a clue." Loud staccato rings blared from a cell phone at his hip. He held it to his ear, his scowl growing deeper with every word. J.D. could have run, but she waited. She watched. Not because of the miles of field or the electrified barbed wire, but because she had come this far. She was going all the way.

She just didn't know how she was ever going to get out.

The man lowered the phone. He stuffed the remote control–size device back into his pocket. "I don't want to hurt you," he repeated, and this time, she suspected he meant, *I've been* ordered *not to hurt you.*

J.D. flexed her fingers. "I don't want to hurt *you.*"

This time, he didn't flinch. But that didn't mean he wasn't afraid.

They stared at each other without speaking, a standoff.

"So now what?" he finally asked, though his voice didn't rise at the end. As if it wasn't a question. As if there could be only one answer.

And — she turned her head again toward the meadow and the twinkling lights of the distant guard posts — there was. "Now I go in."

He came toward her again, as if nothing had happened. She could already feel his fingers digging into her arms, thrusting her forward, at his pace, by his rules. She waved him away.

"Now *I* go in."

He got the message and stepped away. It felt good to give an order, and even better to have it followed. *I can handle this.* She would go inside the windowless building, even though there might be no way out. She would face whatever was waiting for her — would face Ansel Sykes. But she would do it on her own terms, under her own control.

She crossed the parking lot. The man followed behind her, step for step, but he stayed a few feet back. She didn't turn around.

The guards at the door just nodded and swept it open. She barely paused before stepping over the threshold. If she stopped to think, the fear might return.

She was in a long, wide corridor. Everything was a bright, featureless white. And at the end of the hall stood a man.

The first thing she noticed: his shoes, black loafers with a gold bar where the laces would be. The shoes he always wore. Then up, past the gray slacks and the crisp white shirt, the narrow black tie. Up to the bushy eyebrows and the thick glasses, the thin strands of gray hair combed across the leathered bald spot, the grandfatherly smile.

She pressed her lips together, trying not to be sick.

He took a step toward her.

"Dr. Styron," she said, calling him by the name

he had last used. Remembering when she had sat in a cozy office across a desk from him, believing he was looking out for her. And she wanted, more than ever, to vomit.

His lips pretended to smile. "I think it's time you call me by my real name."

She wanted to stay silent, was revolted by the idea of pleasing him. But the words slipped out. "Ansel Sykes."

And his smile grew. "I knew you had it in you."

There was something in his voice, some unexpected note, like . . . pride?

No, that wasn't it. Not quite. It was kind and knowing, with a hint of pride and an undercurrent of cool certainty — and ownership.

It was paternal.

The volcano within her erupted, and the hot flush of anger — of revulsion — took over. Her fingers twitched, from nowhere, the guards appeared, rushed to her, grabbed her, but it made no difference, she would destroy them, destroy them all. Destroy him. This was more than a tingling, more than a spark, this was a lightning bolt splitting her open, charging every inch of her with sizzling, uncontrollable energy.

He was still smiling, and the guards held her arms down, but she didn't need them, she needed only her mind, and she would destroy —

The lights flashed.

Sykes's fingers played over a narrow controller, and a purple glow washed over the white walls, shifting to blue, then green, pulsing rhythmically, in time with her breathing, in time with her heartbeat, and she forgot about Sykes, forgot about the guards, forgot everything but the colors, the colors, the colors, growing, shifting, fading, drawing her in, carrying her away.

"That's all right, she won't hurt me." It was Sykes's voice, and though he hadn't moved, it sounded like he was very far away. "And she's not going any-where, not anymore. Isn't that right?" He gestured to the guards, who dropped their arms and stepped back. And still the lights pulsed, purple then blue then green then purple, and the air thrummed with a low hum, but maybe it was just inside her head. She didn't know.

She didn't care.

The beauty of the lights. The pulsing. The glow. The feeling inside her, welling up, seeping down her legs, down her arms, a numb warmth. *No,* a tiny voice, in the back of her mind. *Fight.*

There was a flash of desire, to move, to run, to spit in his face, to *act,* but it was only a flicker, and then it was gone. Deep inside, she screamed, and then the scream was drowned out by the soft hum. And that, too, was beautiful.

Everything was beautiful, she thought, though it wasn't a thought. There was no thought, not anymore. Only peace. Only calm. Her mind was an ocean, deep and blue and perfectly still. The lights pulsed.

Ansel Sykes stepped toward her, his heels clicking against the floor.

J.D. didn't move. She couldn't move. She wouldn't move.

He clapped her on the shoulder. His hand was heavy and cold. The lights pulsed and flashed and her calm was complete.

"Don't worry, no one can hurt you anymore," he said. "You're safe now."

She smiled, and his face mirrored hers, and it glowed purple, then blue, then green, then purple, and his eyes sparkled in the lights.

"I'm safe now," she repeated, the words floating through her like they belonged to someone else.

"Very good, J.D.," he said, a smile in his voice, and he took her hand and guided her down the corridor, and the lights flashed, and they walked side by side, together, and everything was calm and right and good. "Welcome home."

J.D.'s Race for Answers Ends in a **Pulse-Pounding** Grand Finale!

chasing**yesterday** #3 truth

robin **wasserman**

SCHOLASTIC

Trapped inside the Institute with no place left to run, J.D. comes face-to-face with Dr. Styron—and learns the truth about her past. Now that she knows her destiny, how far will J.D. go to stop it?

SCHOLASTIC
www.scholastic.com

Robin Wasserman remembers almost everything that ever happened to her. She remembers the names of all her teachers and where she sat in their classrooms. She remembers her first goldfish, her pink stuffed elephant, her nursery school nemesis, and the theme song of every TV show she's ever seen. Her friends find this odd. Her parents find it annoying, especially when she interrupts family dinners to say things like, "Remember fourth-grade Halloween when you made me cover up my pixie costume with an ugly brown coat?" But mostly, she remembers good things, which is why she's in no hurry to grow up.

Robin lives in New York City, where she writes books and sometimes rides her bike very fast through the park, pretending she's on a secret mission and being chased by the forces of evil.

As far as she knows, that's just her imagination.

The twists keep coming— and no secrets are safe.

BIG LIES   BIG TROUBLE

Little Secrets

Playing with Fire

EMILY BLAKE

Her mother's in jail. Her best friend betrayed her. Who can Alison trust?

Backstabber Kelly has the world at her feet. Who will she step on next?

Point

Follow Felix On All His Thrilling Adventures!

WISHING FOR MORE THRILLING ADVENTURES?

Children of the Lamp
The Akhenaten Adventure
by P. B. Kerr

Join powerful djinn twins John and Philippa and their eccentric uncle Nimrod on a magical ride to locate a monstrous pharaoh.

Chasing Vermeer
by Blue Balliett

When a priceless Vermeer painting vanishes, two friends find themselves deciphering clues in the middle of an international art scandal, where everyone is suspect.

The Thief Lord
by Cornelia Funke

A magical thriller set among the canals of Venice, where two runaway orphan brothers join a ring of street children led by the mysterious Thief Lord.